SENSING SERAFINA

ELISA ELLIS

CONTENTS

Cover artist: Kat Mellon, Photography by Elisa Ellis, Drawing by Isaac Ellis

Editor: Angie Clarkson

ISBN-13: 978-0-9861187-1-5 (Elisa R Ellis)

✻ Created with Vellum

To my beautiful, crazy, giant family.
I am truly blessed.

Two worlds.
His, hers.
Poor, rich.
Freedom, control.
Until her light breaks through his darkness, bringing them together in a sensory overload. Sera and Cal find love in each other despite their differences until a tragic accident leaves them both in the dark. Will they each be able to overcome personal struggles and adversity to find the light within? And is their love strong enough to withstand the dark?

PART I

Cal

CHAPTER 1

NOW

I feel broken
Cracked.
Tasting blood on my tongue
Glass.
The sight of nothing
Ground.
With the smell of pain
Feelings.
I hear her
Memories.

COVERED IN A FILM OF SWEAT. Thrashing. She's there in my dream, and I don't want to wake up. I can't accept the interruption. Of life. Of living.

Visions in my head. Her hand in mine. She's smiling, her brown hair blowing gently in the wind, a few light freckles so beautifully kissing her porcelain skin. And her eyes. Blue water so clear. I can see myself in them, and I'm glowing, and I've never seen myself like this before. But she keeps fading in and out. Blurry.

"Cal. Cal, you are having a dream. Can you tell me what you are seeing?"

Zaps of light are interfering with my mind, my thoughts that keep trying to hold on to her. I'm resisting consciousness. I want to stay here.

"Cal, you are Ok. Can you talk to me? Tell me what you need?"

The man's voice is grating, patronizing, and fucking infuriating me. Damn it. Just leave me the hell alone. Let me be.

"Cal, you are going to feel a little stick, and then you can relax," I hear the man say.

No. No, not yet. Please leave me here. For a little longer.

But he doesn't, and I fall back into nothingness, somewhere where I don't exist, at least out loud, in my reality. Quiet. My mind is quiet again, and I miss the chaos that I can't reach. It's far away, and I'm floating in nothingness, supposedly resting.

I WAKE up to my mother holding my hand. I know it's her because I can feel her love, but I also feel her strife. I don't like it.

She tries to calm me, to soothe me, but all I can see are a few zaps of light, and frustration, and anger. I don't want to talk, but I have too many questions. Questions I don't really want the answers to. She's still holding my hand rubbing the top of it with her other one, talking, but I don't understand what she's saying. Maybe I don't want to. I hear her, but her words are distorted because I won't allow them to be real in my mind.

I'm searching. Trying to sort things out in my mind. I am restless and pulling away from the hold she has on me, pulling my hand up to my face to find the blindfold that is surely imprisoning my sight. But I'm freaking out. I can't handle the pain, the anguish, the loss. Of my senses. Of my memories. Of my reality.

And then back to silence.

Back and forth. Back and forth. Back and forth. For months.

BEFORE

I park two blocks away because my bike is loud, and her dad won't allow it. I know my marked up skin and idiosyncratic nature is not part of his plan for her life, but I can't stay away.

I stand on the porch, hands in my pockets, a jean jacket hiding my ink, and wait, bouncing a little on my toes in anticipation of her. Her light. The vast inside of her house is cold with shiny, tile floors leading to sterile rooms, too many rooms. It is all-consuming and unforgiving, so much room, but no place to hide from the ever watchful eye of her father, who probably means well.

She opens the door, ready for me. She is bright, yellow, beautiful with bright, white shining all around her like she can't contain her joy. But it is complimentary, not excessive. Just light in every beautiful and perfect way. I am drawn to her like a moth to a flame, like storm to calm.

She yells back to someone that she will be back later and joins me hand in hand, giddy. I don't understand her attraction to me, but I can't allow myself to question it because she is like a drug to me. I am addicted and I can't resist her pull. We walk side by side, so close, touching each other like we are one, our arms weaved together to eliminate any void as we reach my bike.

She jumps onto the back holding me tightly around my middle, and I love that she loves to ride. She loves the wind in her hair, the freedom of the road, and I am thrilled to break her out.

It is only five miles to my house where we plan to study together, only two weeks from graduating and for the plans that we have kept just between us.

But a moment in time, one single second, causes a depression so deep that I can't see recovery.

CHAPTER 2

NOW

One month in, I asked a single time. I couldn't bear to hear it, especially more than once. My mother by my side, I speak low, but surprising her all the same, evident in her jump.

I can't even form it into a full question; her name is enough.

"Sera?"

Just her name on my lips feels blasphemous.

My mother's hesitation affirms my deepest fear. Bandages hide my tears and superficially absorb a shock that sickens me.

Grief so profound consumes my soul. Nothing matters anymore. I don't matter anymore.

I try so hard not to hear her words, but they pierce me, so loud. So, so wrong.

"Baby... She's gone."

BEFORE

Flashes of light. Memories of the only good I have ever known. I turn to them, my only refuge, my only hope of survival.

Before

Hot liquid pools around me, and I recognize only one thing. Despair.

My arm is outreached. Even though my body lies awkwardly displaced, gravel embedding my skin, I strive to feel her presence. I think I hear my voice calling out, but I'm not sure it is really sound.

"Sera?"

Louder. Louder. Louder.

But all I can hear is sirens. Worry. Pain. Extreme pain. And loneliness.

There is shuffling around me. Strangers aiding the impossible but trying anyway.

I finally hear it, a whisper. "Cal." A tone that is so beautiful that it brings hope. Comfort. Praise. Life.

Momentary. Fleeting. But enough that it maintains my heart and saves me. Physically.

CHAPTER 3

NOW

Three, long months of Jell-O, vital checks that interrupted what little sleep I could muster, and the sardonic sterile smell sustaining life but not giving it became my horrible actuality. Merely existing.

Muffled voices in the hall opposite my imprisoning walls portray untouched lives that mock my reality.

I am pushed, forced to get out. I can't leave my pain, but I can at least leave this hell.

I feel the nurse's aid cup the underside of my elbow, leading me as I walk up and down the halls, recovery the goal. Recovery. It is an oxymoron. So insincere and unachievable, always out of grasp. I'm angry, but I press on, determined, and feel my feet shuffle along. In life.

She says, "Good job. Keep going. You are doing great. You've got this." I grumble. Her words are unconvincing, but I must move forward. To endure somehow in this world.

When the doctor removed the bandages, I was unprepared

despite his attempt to warn me. How can something so important be taken for granted without even realizing it? I could feel them moving, searching, my eyes almost jumping to realize their function, but there was nothing.

Darkness.

Sitting in my bed, the pads of my fingers explore my features again, sensing, feeling, my new substitute for sight. I think of how a snake uses his tongue to smell, his senses amiss.

And my hearing. Sounds are louder, more distinct. I have a new recognition as they reverberate, like a bat uses echolocation.

It is inconsistent from what I have always known, and my awareness is heightened. Yet, beauty is nowhere to be found. Pitch black blinds me, robs me along with my loss, but I can't go *there* in my mind, never again.

BEFORE

My eyes follow her around campus, but I haven't put a voice to my feelings for her yet.

The first time I saw her was in the cafeteria. It was like a slow motion movie, the images burning into my mind creating a memory that would last. She stood beside a table of friends, laughing, and brushed her hair back over her shoulder. I immediately wanted to run my own fingers through her light brown, straight hair. I wanted to feel the silk like a child in a store who can't help but touch the beautiful objects on display. She shined among her peers, clearly illuminating her surroundings, and I felt like I couldn't get too close. She would expose me, who I am.

But my determined eyes stayed focused only on her in a room full of noise.

Her hand touched the table, and she shifted to lean on her other leg, again moving her hand to her hair to tuck it behind her ear. And she caught my gaze. She blushed and looked down, but only for a moment before our contact was again established. Across a crowded room.

Her lips turned up just a bit as she tried to discern my stare, but my expression remained unchanged, captivated with her beauty unadorned. A challenge in her eyes forced mine down, defeated by fear and deficiency.

Since that day, I try to blend in to the crowd, hiding from myself. And from her sight. But I see her in my mind even when she is not around.

My mom and I have been on our own since I was born. According to Mom, my angular jaw and deep brown eyes with an olive complexion resemble the *dad* who left at the news of me. It has been a long road, but she has always worked hard to support us, which left me too much time for trouble. Filling my time with the wrong things, bad decisions. Ink covers my skin, telling my story, but revealing a path that has been rough with lessons learned.

I am thankful for my mom, and I don't fault her for my mistakes. It is who we are. But I am discolored, smudged with imperfection. So I can't get too close.

I can't risk blurring the lines, blotting out *her* glow, which is saturated with goodness. So I watch from afar.

I watch her live, my curiosity and intrigue confounding. Every part of her is perfect in an imperfect world, and it's a comfort I've never known before. Bringing color to my pain, she has no idea. It is why she shines. And I can't get enough.

CHAPTER 4

NOW

Waiting for my mom to pull up under the canopy, the cold wheelchair transitions me to freedom. I feel a breeze. It hits my face with calm, taking the sting out of my pain like blowing on a burn. But it's superficial.

The smells of exhaust are overwhelming, reminding me of my loss and the mechanism for my fate.

My feelings, both internal and external, are a tornado, each competing with the other and all trying to overcompensate for a lack of one.

I am wearing sweat pants that hang too loose, a t-shirt, and sunglasses, trusting my mom and the nurse that I look reasonably presentable, but I have my doubts. Thankfully, the ride to my house isn't far, and I don't plan to be out in the open for long. Intimidated by a world I can no longer see.

Feeling my way to the car, I somehow manage to get buckled as the driver of the wheelchair says "good luck." It is contrary to reason.

Mom is excited, though. She tells me she is so happy to get to have me home again, and I can hear the smile in her words, but I can only nod in reply, still conflicted and frustrated. I am happy to reunite with the familiar, though, so I try to embrace this moment in efforts to take one step, one day at a time.

Once home, mom leads me to the front door, which I know to be faded beige, old and dingy. Inside, the smell of home brings tears, and I can't help but release my sadness. I never used to cry. Even when I reaped consequences of stupidity, I never let myself cry, was too tough for it. But now it seems to happen daily, another out-of-control issue that drives me insane.

Mom tries to pretend it isn't happening, not bringing attention to my grief. I think, like me, she wants to pretend it isn't real, that we can just keep moving along like nothing ever happened. But it did. And I hate it.

I remember once when I was around ten, I kept my eyes closed the whole time I took a shower just to see if I could do it. How could I have ever known it would become my reality? I was able to do it that day. I thought at the time that it was kind of fun and relaxing. I never embraced the beauty of the water, the sunlight coming through the window covered with a yellow curtain, the ability to see which bottles contained shampoo and conditioner. Heaven forbid I drop the soap now. I still struggle to find balance. The shower is still a place of refuge for me, though. Standing under the flow of almost too hot water, I try to wash everything away, at least for a while. Kind of reminds me of the line in Macbeth, and I chuckle to myself, sarcastically murmuring, "Out, out damn spot!"

My bed feels wonderful. Ironically, it's the only thing that has improved since my hospital stay. It's a twin bed, the same one I've had all my life and definitely nothing special, but it is heaven compared to the discomfort I've had to deal with for the last three months. I decide to take a nap since there is nothing to do. My days have become full of therapy and nothing. Boredom and indifference.

I realize I will have to rebuild, but apathy is a roadblock trapping me in one spot and preventing any hope of freedom. My mind, when not forced into numbness, is unbearable for right now.

BEFORE

I'm working at a local gas station changing tires and doing some light mechanic work during the Christmas break. I've been working since I was 14, always doing something to make a little extra money since my mom barely kept us afloat. I wear a stained white t-shirt and old jeans, adding new smudges throughout the day. It's comfortable, normal for me. But it feels extremely obvious when she pulls up in her restored 1966 baby blue Ford Bronco, which, by the way, makes me love her a little more.

I wait for her to get out while wiping my hands on the red rag I keep in my pocket, anticipating her needs. Full of life, she hops out. She hesitates when she recognizes me but smiles a timid smile as she asks me about fixing her tire. I don't return her smile. I can't encourage something that has no chance, but my eyes continue to betray me because they will not back down. I hope I don't appear crazy or scary. I honestly can't help it. Can't get enough.

She leaves her tire with me without pushing for conversation, for which I am thankful, but I know she will return to pick it up later, and man, I am burning, consumed with a fire I don't understand. Fire. Hot but dangerous. And my mind is already claiming her as mine.

SHE RETURNS LATER in the day near closing. The sun is setting, and the colors in the sky paint everything around me with a yellow and pink glow, including her hair, causing a reflection of her beauty that is intriguing and persuasive. Again, she smiles, and I am overcome. I hand her the receipt and let my hand brush hers in passing. A spark, a flicker of hope, changes everything. Her eyes meet mine, and an unspoken bond arouses a new direction for me. For us.

CHAPTER 5

NOW

My voice surprises me, the sound louder than expected. Therefore, my few words are spoken quietly. But my legs are covered in bruises and with each time I stumble into something, my harsh words punish my ears, further provoking my frame of mind. I have lived in this apartment with my mom for two years, so navigating the small space doesn't seem like it should be difficult. Mom tried to move things to lessen my challenge, but I'm still learning my way. Through everything.

Today marks one week of being home, and, while I prefer to be here, I'm feeling somewhat claustrophobic. Like cabin fever. I decide to attempt to journey out and ask mom to walk with me to a nearby park. I really hate feeling dependent on her; my loss of independence makes me feel like a child. Hopefully, I can learn new ways to at least get by, but, in my heart, I know there is more for me than that. But I hate waiting. I strive for liberation.

The fresh air feels like a step in that direction, and the smells of the park are comforting and fresh. There is a food cart nearby of which I was already aware, but the scent of food calls me; so, while I wait on a nearby bench, mom buys us a snack. Sitting here with my sunglasses on feels like a disguise, hiding my plight from all passersby. A relief, but misleading even to myself.

The scent of grass and summer heat accented with various flowers and shrubs awakens a small glint of light in my mind. The outdoors have always appealed to me, providing escape, peace, rejuvenation. It is what I need today.

I can hear kids playing, dogs barking, tires of bicycles as they speed by, and somehow my senses provide the image that is lacking, which definitely gives me hope.

It is a long road ahead, but at least I am finally on it.

BEFORE

My schedule changed but I don't care because I don't have many friends at school, nothing and no one relevant to me. I'm just trying to get out of here, so I can leave this town. I don't talk to Mom about my plans. I think she already knows I won't stick around after high school.

I'm not sure what I want to do; I just need fresh air, and it doesn't exist here.

Most of my credits are behind me, so getting out of school early gives me the chance to work, to add to my small savings under my mattress. All I can envision is the open road, my bike. After that, fate will lead the way.

In the back of my mind, though, she lingers, alluring, like a magnet, and her pull is strong.

CHAPTER 6

NOW

Escape. Breaking out of this town has always been my desire, a search for purpose and a fear of monotony. But my residence is within me. And I'm stuck.

My therapist tells me that I'm not trapped. But where can I go from here? In limbo, the battle is real, encompassing, and I can't see to get out. I want to surrender and wave the white flag, to concede to the darkness. Rescue is an illusion, a mirage that I stumble to reach. So I settle for contentment; yet, even it is still fleeting.

Never participating in many activities while growing up, I lean on the one thing I enjoyed, in which I found some sense of fulfillment and placation. My hands provide in me a truce, a medium for expression. Sculpting, a lifeline, a means to escape, but also to remain.

I had two weeks remaining in my high school career when fate circumvented everything, effectively extinguishing my life with her, turning our dreams into fantasy. I still graduated on paper; the school generously exempted my finals, my previous grades enough to pass, and my therapist, Dr. Roberts, encouraged me to attend the local junior college in the field of art. While school was never something I wanted to pursue long term, art has never felt like work. The most difficult aspect of going would be using the necessary resources and accommodations per my disability, a huge dent in my already scarred pride.

A couple of days ago, I decided to explore the idea of at least taking a few classes. It is a start.

I made a call to the college and spoke with someone in the admissions department who directed me to a guidance counselor, Mrs. Penny Peterson. Apparently, "there are a handful of blind students who are very successful." She arranged for a meeting to help me with the application process and to direct me towards a "wonderful college experience." Her cheeriness was preferable to the alternative, but she was clearly disillusioned to my struggle. I tried to humor her, putting on a mask of togetherness and ability despite my lack of confidence internally.

"Are you sure you don't want me to go in there with you?" my mom asks after leading me to the appropriate door to the administration building. It is a small college that boasts small classes and personal attention. I appreciate the smaller campus and fewer buildings to maneuver.

"No. I will figure it out on my own," I answer her, partly continuing to be a martyr, though I wouldn't admit that aloud, and partly as a test. It's like a baby bird learning to fly, the mom coaxing it out of the nest, even though falling to the ground a few times is imminent. I have to embrace instinct. If I had been born this way, it would be my normal. I would know nothing else. But I wasn't, and no amount of nurturing will teach me to survive.

I'm using my walking cane, listening intently to my surroundings when I hear my counselor approach me. She had agreed to meet me just inside the double doors of the building.

"Cal? I'm Mrs. Peterson, but you can call me Mrs. Penny. Everyone else does." I feel her hand on my shoulder and try not to wince, hoping that one day unexpected touch will seem less shocking.

Attempting a smile, I extend my right hand in the direction of her voice. "Nice to meet you."

To prevent an opportunity for awkwardness, she quickly continues, "Well Ok, let's get you started. If it's ok with you, I will lead you to my office."

I try so hard to ignore the *difference* in the way people talk to me, *handle* me. It sounds like Mrs. Peterson is not new to assisting people like me, but I still notice a hint of sympathy and possibly the notion that she takes pride in helping the unfortunate. I hope I'm mistaken. Just jumping to conclusions to preempt possible truths that might destroy my psyche even more.

She places my hand on her elbow. I wonder if she thinks about how it feels to me. I can hear her age in her voice, but the soft, smooth skin of her exposed elbow further proves her appearance, the loose skin reflecting years beyond mine or even my mom's.

Walking slowly, my feet shuffle beside, but a little behind her, and I hear people glide past us at a normal pace, their air breezing by me, unaffected and unaware. I think of the cliché *ignorance is bliss*, recognizing its own irony.

Finally seated, I hear Mrs. Peterson shuffle some papers and walk around her desk before sitting in her chair that I can hear deflate and then squeak as it reclines beneath her weight.

She explains the process and places my hand where signatures are required. I think about the trust necessary, my mind considering bizarre scenarios where I could have signed my rights away.

"Do you have any questions, Cal?"

"So, you said I will receive a guided tour before classes start?" I ask, my fear creeping back in, a constant shadow greedily lurking behind my ambition.

"Yes, yes. Let me see if Lexi is around. She could take you around campus right now if you like?" She ends her sentence on an up note, in the form of a question. "It's actually a good time to do it if you have time because most of the students have not arrived for fall semester yet and the last summer session is wrapping up." Time. An overstated abundance that is currently my adversary.

I think of Mom waiting in the car and decline the offer, my fear the victor this time.

"Thank you, but I might just have my mom help me find my way around sometime this week. I appreciate your time, Mrs. Peterson," I say, standing and looking forward to the completion of a mentally exhausting but encouraging meeting.

"Mrs. Penny. Call me Mrs. Penny. Let me help you to the door," she says.

"Mrs. Penny. Right. Thank you."

Once outside the building, I search the sounds around me and wait, knowing my mom will be watching for my exit. I hear the car door shut, the old, creaking sound distinct with rust, and hear mom's footsteps rushing to my aid. I know she means well. But it still sucks.

BEFORE

I attend a large school, which makes it easy to blend in and kind of disappear into the pandemonium within the halls between classes. I'm pretty quiet and don't feel the need to fit in. I contradict the stereotypical high school student, refusing to conform. I also don't want to be viewed as the cool deviant. I guess, really, I just prefer to remain inconspicuous, for now.

Except for when I see her standing near the door that leads to the student parking lot, the door I need to exit so I can head to work. I don't pay to park in the student lot, but my motorcycle fits easily along the adjacent residential street. I see her before she sees me. She appears to be waiting for someone, and I wonder if she is leaving early like me. I know she is a senior because her ID badge is purple like mine, a classification method used to help the faculty keep track.

I slow down my walk, giving myself a little more time to observe her unaware. *God, she is beautiful.* My attraction to her is primal, compelling, destined.

Turning around, she sees me and stills, recognizing this gravitation we seem to share. A hint of a smile illuminates the direct path I follow towards her, commanding my steps. The space between us, close. I decide I can't contain my thoughts, so I allow myself a few words hoping the rest won't spill out, not prepared to reveal the overwhelming feelings I have for a girl to whom I haven't even spoken yet.

"Are you waiting for someone?" I ask.

But she doesn't answer my question, her own out before I can finish mine.

"Are you leaving early?" she asks.

Both of our grins widen and my hand falls from the door, not ready to open it yet. I answer her first, "I'm finished for the day, so I was headed to work. You?"

"Yeah, me, too. Except for the work part. But yeah, I'm finished for the day."

"So, I didn't get your name the other day. At the shop."

"Sera. It's short for Seraphina, but I just go by Sera. And yours?"

"It's good to finally meet you, Sera," I say, taking her hand in mine to shake it, but I maintain our hold, answering her, "I'm Cal." This moment, while out of my norm, somehow still fits into my comfort zone. As we sift through the initial awkward introductions, it feels like there is still a calm and compatible harmony between us.

"Nice to meet you, too, Cal." My name on her lips, her smile, the light behind her eyes, the feelings I have ~ sensory overload. And I am done, intoxicated, complete.

She looks at our hands, and I realize I haven't released hers, so I let go and feel immediately cool, desperate to regain the warmth she brings me. I can tell she feels it, too, her mouth falling, afflicted.

"Maybe I will see you again soon?" I say, not ready to leave.

"Definitely," she assures me. "Soon," she says, smiling again. I smile back and head out the door, already counting the hours until we meet again.

CHAPTER 7

NOW

I feel relief when the sun moves behind the clouds, the burn on my arms and face easing. August heat causes my sunglasses to slide down my nose, my sweat frustrating me. A drought smothers our state, stunting new growth and denying liquid nourishment. The burnt grass mixes with the hot air and slaps me, hits me head on, while I slowly walk the campus with my mom, feeling out my future path.

I labor through it, anticipating the reward, the light at the end of the tunnel.

Mom encourages me. "I'm proud of you, Cal."

I mutter, "Thanks." Conflicted. I need her help, her approval, but I look forward to doing this on my own. "I can do this," I keep telling myself but seeing is believing and I have to find a new avenue for belief. My destination suspended in faith.

After several walks that orient me to the campus, we stop at the local ice cream place. I've always had a thing for pistachio ice cream, and Mom is determined to lighten the mood. It's a treat we don't often get. The texture, cold and creamy with the crunchy nuts mixed in, is more noticeable to me now, and I'm able to enjoy it in a new way.

The bell on the door rings as a group of kids come in; they are all talking enthusiastically about what flavors they want. But I notice a sudden hush, followed by a mom's whisper, "It's not nice to point." Several minutes later, their topic changes and the kids are talking about a t-ball game, which I assume preceded their trip here.

Mom puts her hand on mine. She recognizes my pause when I hear their conversation. I know they are pointing at me, at the scars that I can feel when I touch my head. Sunglasses unable to mask the raw, jagged lines that map the accident, which now serve as another constant reminder. Wounds I try not to notice when I run my hand through my messy, brown hair, a habit that is hard to break. But I guess I don't care what they think about me. It is insignificant. I will get used to it. Eventually.

Right now, art is my light. I embrace the ability to lose myself while creating something beautiful, something that represents what I can no longer reach. It is a substitute that will sustain me.

BEFORE

My favorite part of each day: Sera standing by the door. But after a week of exchanging smiles and goodbyes, I need more.

I notice as I near the door, Sera is watching me.

I feel myself smile, and I look forward to her, to any interaction with her.

"Hi again," I say, approaching her at the end of the hall, just inside the double doors where she usually stands.

"Hey, Cal. You headed to work?"

"Actually, no, not today. Got the day off."

"Oh, that's cool," she smiles back, our usual small conversation having become the norm.

"Yeah, it's good. So, what are you up to today?" I ask, hoping to extend my time with her, even if only for a few minutes while we talk.

"Oh, me? Just headed home I guess. Sometimes I stop at the library, but I don't have any homework today, which is nice."

"It's pretty today, especially for this time of year." I hesitate but decide I have to just put it out there. "Would you, uh, want to hang out at the park for a little while?" I bite my bottom lip and have to force my hands to be still by my side. I don't know why I'm so nervous. Maybe it's that I know how much I like her already, how much I would have to lose if she says no.

"Umm, sure. Yeah... just let me text my dad and let him know what I'm doing. He kind of freaks out if I don't," she smiles, getting her phone out.

"Definitely." It takes about a minute for her dad to respond, but it feels like too long for that little swoosh sound that means so much. Looking down at her phone, she grins and nods at me.

My smile widens. And my nerves dissipate. "Let's go," I say, grabbing her hand with a new sense of confidence. In me. In us. Our future that I know is imminent.

Her giggle is kindle, rousing a new relationship full of beauty. Attraction. Her brilliance, my calling.

I walk her to my bike and hand her my only helmet. "Put this on." She takes it, and I have to help her with the buckle under her chin. I ask, "Have you ever ridden before?" I can see she is unsure.

"No. Is it scary?" She is so innocent, adorable. I chuckle. "No, it's not scary. You will love it; trust me. Just hold on to my jacket." She nods at me and her eyes reflect faith. Something new and uncharted for me. It's exhilarating.

I drive slowly and carefully, and I can tell she wants more, her joy evident in her laugh. I love getting to be the one who introduces her to the spontaneity, the weightlessness of riding. It is the closest thing to flying. A satisfaction unmatched. Until her.

We drive around the park to a spot where ducks are swimming in a small lake. There is a monumental, old tree, its branches providing protection over a perfect moment where we sit on its roots facing the water.

Looking at me, she grins, "You were right; it's not scary. In fact, I loved riding with you. It's so freeing."

"Yeah, it brings me peace, the wind on my face, even the loud sound of my bike. It's like it's drowning out all of the other noises." I feel a little exposed sharing this, worried I sound too intense, so I pick at the grass nearby, not making eye contact.

"You're right. I felt like it was all there is, like I have no worries."

I glance up to see her looking at me, smiling, encouraging.

My lips turn upward and our eyes lock for a second, long enough to see each other more clearly. Revealing a connection deeper than either of us can understand. A door opening to a scene so serene, vibrant, jubilant, but stepping through requires a leap. Over my fears. Over my inhibitions. But my legs are running in my mind, getting a good start so I can clear the fissure dividing us.

I jump.

CHAPTER 8

NOW

Two weeks of classes and I'm finally feeling more confident about getting around and adjusting to college life despite my disability. I have to immerse myself and allow everything to sink in. My previous style of learning was seeing the information. I would commit things to memory visually. Maybe that is helping me now. I can still visualize the material, although it may not be completely accurate. It helps me to stay sane though. I can't let darkness invade my spirit just because it took my eyes.

I'm taking four different classes, two art classes and two basic prerequisites necessary for any degree. I decided I might as well obtain a degree if I'm going to bother with attending college. Freshman English and Algebra are easy for me. They always were. Mrs. Penny connected me with the financial aid department, and I was given a grant to help cover my classes and supplies. I was able to use it to get a laptop that, with new technology, allows me to hear what I can't read. I'm still learning braille; it's not coming easily to me. I also have a special calculator that assists me in algebra.

I'm surrounded by voices and sounds, though, something through which I constantly have to sift in order to find what is relevant. Sometimes it is very distracting, especially for me. Growing up, I frequently became lost in thought, easily losing focus. Now, every single sound has to be intentionally discarded. A sneeze, a cough, a giggle, paper shuffling, pencils dropping, the click of the teacher's shoes as she walks and teaches at the same time, the hum of the lights, a yawn.

My art classes are better. Entering the art department, I am comforted by the smell of clay, acrylic paint, lacquer, and pencil shavings. A smell of creativity. A sense of belonging as I enter my realm. The first couple of weeks have been spent on basics, and this week, we finally begin to work on our first project. The class is small with about fifteen students, probably only half who are serious. To my left is Ray. He speaks quietly but is worth hearing. I have to pay close attention, but his intelligent and dry sense of humor is a relief to the frustrations of the day. He doesn't treat me differently, even teasing me about my situation. At first, I was taken aback, but I appreciate it now.

"Dude! Watch what you are doing," he tells me. My initial internal response is sarcastic and irritated, but he continues, and I realize it's what I need.

"Whatever, man. Why don't you get up and help me?" I knocked over a glass of water that is for cleaning tools. I have it at my table so that I don't have to waste time going back and forth to the sink, but obviously it isn't very helpful at the moment. He puts paper towel in my hand telling me, "Nah, looks like you've got this." I sigh in response, but inside, I'm thankful for the opportunity to be forced to do something so simple, yet significant to me.

After my table is once again dry, Ray asks, "What are you making for your project?"

"You can see it better than me," I respond, deciding I might as well make light of my situation.

"Ha ha. Yeah, that would help if it actually looked like something," he jokes back.

I chuckle and answer, "Well, you will be able to tell what it is soon enough," continuing to keep my project private. I think I just want to wait until it takes shape before declaring what it is. I have an idea of what I want it to be, but it takes time to actually form it, and I wouldn't be able to do it justice with words.

"Fine. I guess we will all see later, that is, if you can make it more obvious than the big lump it is right now."

"Are you telling me that your project is already finished?" I ask him, skeptical that it will be very good if so.

"Nah. It still needs the finishing touches. It's coming right along, though," he reassures me.

"Cool. When you are done, let me feel it and see if I can tell that it is even a skull. I'm betting it will feel more like an apple with holes in it." He's been talking about making a sugar skull since we are sculpting with clay for our first project.

"Shut up. You'll see. Or not," he jokes.

I feel my jaw clench, knowing he is teasing, but feeling frustrated that I won't be able to actually see it. I tell myself it isn't worth seeing it anyway. My project will be more abstract. Intentionally.

"You just crack yourself up, huh? Stupid asshole."

We both laugh, continuing to work and talk a little here and there.

BEFORE

Hanging out with Sera at the park is a new beginning, a seed sure to blossom into glory. Each time our eyes meet, I hear her laugh, or we just sit silently together, it sprouts something more. Growing peace, beauty, comfort, ecstasy. Love.

We have been seeing each other for three weeks now, but our meetings are limited. I work most days, and Sera's dad is not a fan of her having a boyfriend, or even a friend who is a boy. Her mother passed away when she was seven, so her dad is close to her, but also very protective. She doesn't want to disappoint him. His new wife is just a distraction, unable to completely fill the void that was Sera's mother, and he can't lose what he has left. I hate it for them, but I wish he could loosen his hold, allow her room to live her own life. Sera stayed within her boundaries before meeting me, and I can see her desire to explore, to flourish. Her light is too strong to be hidden.

I fear my ability to provide her what she seeks, but I'm willing to take the chance.

We had planned to meet after I got off work tonight at nine, but I've already been waiting twenty minutes and she isn't here. I sit alone in a booth inside a local restaurant in our small town. It is open until 10:30 since it's a Friday, but it's already empty and the waitresses are finishing up their end-of-night tasks to prepare for the large expected Saturday crowd they have every week for breakfast. One waitress, Marge, a lady in her sixties, has worked here ever since I can remember. She is wiping tables down and refilling salt and pepper shakers while another younger waitress is vacuuming the short-piled carpet covered in various colors that reflect the 70s, stains blending in perfectly. I notice her glance at me several times, probably ready to go home, my preventing their closing.

Marge finally comes over to my table and leans on the opposite booth. "Hey, Cal." She looks at her large-faced watch and back at me, hoping I will explain myself.

"Hi, Marge. Sorry. I'll get out of your way," I say, getting up and grabbing my cap.

"I don't mean to rush you, honey. But I think you may be waiting here all night by yourself," she says, looking at the door like it's confirmation.

"Yeah, it's ok. I was just leaving." I don't plan to explain anything to her. She is a nice lady, but I don't want my life being discussed at tomorrow's breakfast any more than it already will, speculation of my waiting alone sure to come up at some point.

I've already texted Sera a few times, wondering what happened.

Resigned, I get on my bike to head home when I feel my phone buzz in my pocket just before starting it up.

"I'm so sorry. My dad got home late from work and insisted I stay and eat dinner with him. I still really want to see you. Any chance you could come over here?" I read her message and smile, despite her situation.

She wants to see me. That's all that matters to me right now. I quickly hit the kickstand with the back of my foot and crank up the bike. I text her back, "I'm on my way."

It only takes about five minutes to arrive and park in front of her large house. Intimidated enough by just going in and definitely about meeting her dad, I wipe my hands on my jeans. I head up the walkway anticipating shaking his hand and I don't want to make a bad impression with sweaty hands, evidence of my nerves. I lift my shoulders and stand up straight, trying to exude the confidence I'm lacking and knock on the door.

Her father answers. "Hello. You must be Cal. I'm Henry," he says, shaking my hand firmly. I respond in kind, "It's nice to meet you, Sir." He hesitates before letting me pass, and I notice his eyes on my bike.

"Is that your motorcycle?"

I turn back to look at my bike even though I know mine is the only one parked in front of the house and nod as I look back at him again.

"Doesn't seem very safe," he states, like he can somehow influence me.

"It's not bad. I'm careful." I don't care about me. But I am careful when Sera is with me.

Thankfully, Sera comes around the corner smiling brightly. She hugs me and welcomes me in. I would love nothing more than holding her in that hug forever, but with Henry standing next to us, I let her go and follow her to sit next to her on a floral couch that looks like it is never used. A large Oriental rug adorns the hardwood floor, on top of it a granite-topped coffee table heavy enough to indent the four corners where the decorative, wooden feet rest. A piano stands against one wall, a picture window on the adjacent wall. The room opens to a foyer, and stairs meet in the middle guided by shined, cherry wooden bannisters. I've seen enough to recognize I don't belong.

My mom and I live in a two-bedroom apartment where we share a bathroom with a small shower. Our small, plain kitchen provides well enough with an attached dining area that leads into our square-shaped living room. We have an old couch and two blue recliners that have seen better days, but are comfortable. A brown and gold metal TV tray serves as a table between the chairs that sit facing our 19 inch box tv. Clearly, our unassuming home is no match for the beautiful abode where I sit across from Henry. Sera sits next to me with one foot under her, leaning into me innocently, unaware of the glare I can feel from her father.

He doesn't seem angry, just concerned, like he needs to protect Sera from me. Ironically, though, I feel the same desire to protect Sera. From everything, including him. Like it's my job now, because she is mine.

The room is quiet, so our voices sound a little too loud causing the awkward silence to extend even with the sound of our conversation.

Henry crosses one leg over the other and addresses me: "I understand you are a senior like my Sera here. What are your plans for after you graduate?"

I'm sure nothing short of an Ivy League school would impress him, and I especially don't want to tell him I had planned to travel on my bike and take a year to just kind of find myself. "I haven't decided, Sir," I say, thinking that's the best response I can think to give.

"Oh. Well, ok. I hope you figure it out pretty soon. Graduation is just around the corner."

I nod to acknowledge him, thinking I can't wait. I can't wait to get out of this town. I want to explore, not just other places, but also who I am. I'm searching for purpose, for freedom, for my life.

Sera wraps her hand around my arm in a reassuring way. We haven't discussed our futures, but I sense her need for the same things. But her dad is important to her, and I don't know if she can break away. I really hope so because, even after a short time with her, I don't know if I can find what I'm looking for without her by my side. The door is before me, but she is the key.

To me.

CHAPTER 9

NOW

Molding clay, the cool and silky material forms beneath my hands therapeutically. We are still working on our first project in art. On the first day, Mr. Kenan gave us a syllabus describing the objective for this class: to create a collection of pieces using multiple media that express one emotion. Each student's interpretation of the assignment is considered valid and, with the instructor's guidance, we are to use different materials to build multiple projects that relate to one theme. Everyone uses clay for the first project, and I've heard students discussing their themes with each other. Death, love, seasons, school. Most of the ideas sound superficial, which isn't surprising considering the majority of my classmates live typical college lives, none of them having gone through life-changing experiences or anything too deep. I've continued to remain quiet regarding my plan. Words inadequate and too revealing.

Mr. Kenan has agreed to teach me, intrigued by my desire to create despite my lack of sight. Most of the classes already have some sort of protocol for disabled students, but according to Mrs. Penny, art wasn't one of them. My initial response: irritation. Am I supposed to be thankful? Feel indebted? My sarcasm, a tyrannical vehicle recklessly guarding my insecurities. But when Mr. Kenan introduced himself to me prior to the first class, he surprised me.

"I've heard a lot about you, Cal. It's very nice to meet you," he said, shaking my hand.

I nodded in response, still wishing for normal.

"I appreciate your desire to learn art, Cal, but let me just tell you now, I won't baby you. You are expected to perform just like everyone else. I will not make accommodations on assignments or grading. If you feel like you can't keep up, you are welcome to drop the course."

"I'm not too worried about that, Mr. Kenan. See you in class," I said, a small smile acknowledging his challenge.

He's been true to his word so far. I hear him occasionally walk around checking on students and their progress. As he nears my desk, he sighs.

"This project needs to be completed in the next two weeks, Cal. If you keep adding clay, you won't have time to finish."

"Yes, sir."

My short response frustrates him. He reiterates, "If you can't complete this project on time, your grade will suffer."

"I understand, sir."

He concedes, sighing as he moves to the next student. We are allowed to work in the lab during open times, and considering I have nothing better to do, I am here more than not. I easily stay ahead in my other classes, finishing assignments as soon as I can. It's almost like a competition within myself. A means to prove my competence. Plus, time is all I have right now. It seems like it's never-ending. Like the movie *Groundhog Day* in my mind as I relive my loss on an automatic track. Beauty, beginning, life, tragedy, loss, darkness. Again and again and again. I don't know if I'm just afraid losing memories will end me or if I'm already gone. A six-month period defining my entire life.

So I try to trick my mind. I fill it with homework, music, art, whatever I can find to avoid the screams of the silence of my future.

Ray laughs at my short responses to Mr. Kenan. "I told you. Mr. Kenan can't even tell what you're doing."

"Shut up, man. Creativity takes time," I say, smirking.

"Yeah, yeah. We'll see, I guess. Hey, why don't you hang with some of the guys and me at *Triple Eight* tonight? We're going to have a few beers, play pool, just chill."

"How are you planning to drink? You're only 19," I remind him.

"I've got my ways. Anyway, you need to get out more. You're gonna turn into some kind of freak hermit, all pale and creepy, if you don't," he teases.

"Whatever. I'd rather be a hermit than a douchebag like you," I joke back.

Ignoring my comeback, he keeps on, "Seriously, man. You wanna come? I can pick you up."

"Sure. I guess."

I'm nervous. I wasn't exactly a social person even before my accident. But, then again, I'm not that person anymore anyway. Might as well try it. I definitely wouldn't mind having a few beers. Mom refuses to buy them for me, not because of my age, but because she remembers how I used to be. Before I met Sera.

I just want to escape though. Pretend I'm like a normal college kid doing normal college things.

BEFORE

Since we have to be so careful around Sera's dad, she told him she was spending the night with a friend on Friday so that we can go on a date. Her friend had already invited her to a party, so it's not too much of a stretch. I'm just going to go to the party with them. I'm not sure this party is for me, though.

I'm used to partying. Hanging out with the guys, smoking, drinking, behind where I work. There is a slab back there where a few of

39

us from work sit talking, listening to music. I tend to lose myself there. My life drowned out and my mind, free in spirit, calm. Away from the stresses of what I don't have, far from the chores that are necessary for my mom and me to live. It's all I've really known, this fight to live a life not worth much.

But tonight is different. With Sera, the fight has become real.

I arrive at Sera's friend's house at 7:50. Ten minutes early. Hoping it doesn't matter, I knock on the large wooden door and wait. I notice the intricate designs carved deep into the grain of the dark wood, majestic-looking as if it serves a higher purpose than just an entrance. With iron accents, this door is a boundary, a gate separating the meek from the strong, and I'm on the wrong side. Its beauty is enchanting. I am lost in thought when it opens, startling me a little.

I am greeted with a smile from a woman in her 50s, assumedly Chasity's mom. Sera has introduced me to Chasity before, and she looks like the woman before me.

"Hi. I'm Cal. I was supposed to meet Chasity and Sera here?" I say, a bit nervously.

"Hi, Cal. Well aren't you something special? Come in and keep me company. I'm sure the girls will be down in a minute."

"Thank you, ma'am." Forced to duck under her arm as she leans on the doorway motioning me in, I smell alcohol on her breath. She puts her arm around me, closing the large door behind her, and escorts me to a dark red, leather couch in front of a huge fireplace.

"We can wait here in the den. It's more cozy in here, don't you think, Cal?"

"Yes ma'am. Thank you." I sit down on one end of the couch in effort to leave plenty of room for her. Before she sits, she pours two glasses of what looks like scotch from a decanter and insists I drink up as she sits too closely to me, our legs touching.

I try to scoot a little further away, but there isn't anywhere to go without being rude, so I take the glass and sip. She places her hand at the end of my glass and encourages me to down it, so I do. She smiles and places her hand on my thigh.

"So, Cal, how did the girls find *you*?"

"I'm not sure what you mean exactly, ma'am. We all go to school together."

I am not interested. She's not the first woman who has pursued me. I've had many ladies flirt with me when they bring their cars into the shop. They act innocent, like they need rescuing or something. Like I'm some kind of bad boy, someone they can have as their guilty pleasure. She doesn't seem to understand I'm taken.

I remove her hand from my thigh and stand up to look at the large amount of hunting trophies adorning the walls. I don't really admire them, but I hope they can create enough of a distraction to prevent further interaction with her. Sadly, I think she is probably just another trophy for the man who keeps this collection, everything about her fake and doctored, even her personality.

She's not deterred, unfortunately. I feel her too close behind me and she reaches around my waist, like I'm a toy specially made for her. Grabbing her hand, I turn around and redirect her to sit back down.

"Ma'am. Thank you for having me in your home. I'm going to text Sera and see if they are about ready yet."

She frowns playfully, not ready to give up, but I remain standing while I text Sera:

"Babe, are y'all about ready? I'm kind of under attack down here."

"What? Yeah, coming down now," she responds.

I hear them giggling as they come down the stairs, and my eyes are drawn to her. She is stunning in a pale green sundress that falls above her knees and accentuates her curves, beautifully bringing out the small, green flecks in her blue eyes. I smile, watching her descend as I walk to meet her, grabbing her into a tight hug when we meet.

"Hey. Thanks for rescuing me. You look great," I whisper into her hair.

A gorgeous smile on her face, she whispers back, "From what, babe?"

"The cougar," I whisper back and briefly look at Chasity's mom. They don't notice, busy talking to each other.

Sera giggles, "I bet you can hold your own. You're pretty tough." She grabs my hand so that we can get Chasity and leave, and I squeeze her hand, winking at her. "You know it, babe." I'm glad she isn't reacting weirdly. Maybe she knew Chasity's mom is like this? Either way, I'm thankful she recognizes my honor, that I would never do anything to hurt her, even when under attack by a cougar.

Chasity drives a little sports car so we have to go in Sera's Bronco. I'm driving while they chat. This car is badass so I don't mind. The party is about thirty miles away in an extremely wealthy subdivision. I've driven by but never entered the gated community; so, as I pull up to the gate, the girls instruct me to enter in a code. I guess that's one way of making sure only the invited are able to attend. Except I'm not invited. I hope it won't be an issue. I'm not sure I have enough tolerance to deal with a bunch of dumbass preps.

I drive around a couple of curvy streets before parking along the side of the wide road that sits between mansions. There are about twenty or so cars already parked closer to the house, which the girls point out as the party house. It is all lit up, and I can hear the music playing and people laughing as we walk about a block and a half to get there. I assume there are no parents around. It looks like there are teenagers just making themselves at home throughout the inside and outside of the house, but they do look older, I think only juniors and seniors in the mix. I vaguely recognize a few guys from some of my classes, but I generally keep to myself in school so I don't figure they will talk to me.

Wearing my worn jeans with a plain black t-shirt, I feel out of place, but Sera is holding my hand tightly as we weave in and out of the crowd. She doesn't seem to be worried about being here with me. I wish I was that sure. I'm a confident person, but I'm not naive. I recognize the difference between me and the rest of the people here. Money makes a big difference in this world, and I'm not a part of the big-money club. It's cool with me, but I doubt it is with them as I notice the people who aren't flat out ignoring me, give me looks of disdain.

Chasity screams with excitement as we come up on a group of their friends. There are three girls and two guys who all hug Sera and Chasity when we approach them. As Sera introduces me, they all seem nice, the girls smiling and guys shaking my hand. We each grabbed a beer from a keg on the way through the backyard. I'm wishing I already had another, just a bit to put me more at ease. It's hard to match Sera's light. Her radiant aura is so serene; I don't want the storm in my mind clouding this night. Just being with her, near her, I feel joy. She smells sweet, delicious. I move closer, pulling her in front of me so that I can wrap my arms around her and keep her close, and I feel her push back against me. It is soothing and intense at the same time. Just between us.

Surrounded by laughter and kids playing beer pong, music adding to the background noise, we are still in our own little moment. Swaying to the sounds, our energy combined fills up a space bigger than us, love almost overflowing, like fizz that barely stays contained within its cup. I talk quietly into her ear, feeling her soft hair against my lips.

"I love being here with you. Thank you for inviting me."

Turning her head back into my chest so that I can see her smile, she says, "It's so pretty tonight. I wouldn't want to be anywhere else but right here in your arms."

"Same here." She feels like home to me. Warm and inviting. Comfort but chaos at the same time, my senses intertwining, creating sparks on the verge of a blaze.

We are so caught up in ourselves that we don't see the idiot who's coming towards us before he's already up in my face, sloshing his damn beer onto my legs and shoes.

"What do you think you're doing here? Why don't you go back to your little shack where you belong?"

"What the hell, man? What's your fucking problem?" I yell back at him.

Sera is trying to pull me away. "Babe, babe, let's just go. C'mon. He's not worth it."

I'm clenching my jaws together, tense and infuriated at the interruption. I don't even care what he thinks about me, but he's not going to ruin this night. I won't let him. And as much as I don't want to hurt Sera, I also refuse to stand down, not to this asshole.

"My problem is you; I don't think a poor, white trash, trailer park piece of shit like you deserves to be here, and you sure don't deserve to touch Sera."

Sera yells, "You're drunk Chance. Just leave us alone."

I can't help it, though. I'm done. I punch him in the jaw and the fight is on. He swings back but misses, clearly impaired, so I bend down and pick him up just to throw him back down on the ground. I'm on top of him punching him in the face repeatedly for who knows how long before several guys grab me to pull me off of him. I vaguely remember Sera screaming in the background, begging me to stop, but I can't stop. I notice he's out when I'm standing up, backing away while everyone is still around me, just watching. Cell phones out, documenting my every move which makes me sick. I'm not their toy, their entertainment for the night. I hate the permanency of the internet and don't look forward to school next week, sure I'll hear about it.

I mean, sure, the few people who know me will congratulate me for kicking his ass, the stupid prick deserving, but I don't want that for Sera.

I stand beside her Bronco, still heated in fury, but it's coming down hard as my adrenaline rush dissipates, leaving me drained and frustrated with my reaction. I hate that I scared Sera. She's probably disgusted with me. I'm just about to start walking back into town when I hear her call out to me.

"Cal. Wait up."

I look down while wringing my hands and kind of walk in a circle trying to decide how to talk to her. But before I talk, she's already talking and I'm trying to catch up, my mind still in another place.

"Babe, wait. I'm sorry. I'm so sorry about Chance. He just doesn't understand."

I speak calmly, trying hard to subdue the wrath I have just hearing his name, much less the fact that she's the one apologizing to me.

"No. Stop. I'm sorry. I don't know why I let him get to me," still conflicted about what the appropriate reaction would have been. Honestly, it felt good to beat the shit out of him. Sometimes I want to fight someone just for the hell of it anyway, so his coming at me was a good excuse to let go. But I shake my head. I don't want to be *them*. I don't want to conform. And she's one of them, so I'm unsure what to do. What does she want from me?

Her hands hold my face lovingly, bringing me back to where she is, and it's good. She's good. I can feel her spirit, and her kindness envelops mine.

I place my roughed-up hands on top of hers, caressing her with my thumbs while releasing my pain and holding on for dear life. She is my life. Words aren't necessary and I'm grabbing her, embracing her, leaving no space for anything to get between us.

"Babe," I sigh. "Thank you. Thank you for believing in me. I'm so sorry." I can't stop apologizing to her, convincing her of my worth. Convincing myself.

"It's ok. Really, it's ok, Cal. Let's just get in the car. I'll text Chasity and tell her to hurry up and come on."

"Ok." It's all I can say.

We wait for about fifteen minutes for Chasity, and I'm about ready to lose it. I don't want to be anywhere near this overpriced neighborhood anymore, surely filled with more *Chances*. I've never been more proud to be poor because right now, I have more than ever, more than anyone else here. I have Sera, and I have hope. A fortune worth more than any material thing. It's then that I realize Chance's problem.

"Babe, were you with him? Did you date Chance before me?"

45

She looks down, embarrassment shadowing her glow, and I hate it. She nods, a tear falling before she can catch it.

"I'm sorry. I'm not mad. It just explains why. That's all." I can't be mad at her. If anything, I'm sorry she was ever subjected to his toxic attitude. He's fake, but tonight the masks were gone, and his ugliness overtook his features, distorted with each word out of his mouth.

Pulling at a small string on her dress, she remains uncomfortable while she talks. "It's not ok, though, Cal. I can't believe he said that stuff. What a jerk! I mean, I don't know what kind of claim he thinks he has on me. What right does he have to even say anything at all?"

I love her. She is so pure. She doesn't see the evil in this world, and I want to shelter her from it for the rest of our lives. I will not let this happen again. She will never see me in a rage like that again. I have to be who she needs me to be.

"Come here," I tell her, reaching to pull her into my arms across the console between us. "It's ok. It won't happen again, and we are ok. Right?" I cup her face, bringing her eyes to mine. "Right?"

She nods, and I'm thankful.

Chasity jumps in the car breaking up our little moment.

"Hey guys!" She talks too loudly. Out of breath, overly excited. "Well that was crazy, huh?"

"Seriously, Chasity?" Sera asks, frustrated at her friend's shallow disposition.

"What? You should have seen everybody in there after y'all left!"

"Why? What happened?" I ask, unfortunately too curious for my own good.

"Well, Chance is fine, but he's pissed. A couple of guys tried to help him up but he didn't want their help and stormed off into the house. I could hear people talking, and most of them sounded like they were glad Chance finally got his ass kicked."

"Really?" I ask, sarcastically and disbelieving.

"Yeah, well, I mean, they weren't exactly siding with you, but still, I think a lot of our friends are sick of Chance. He can be a real jerk to everyone. But, yeah, some of them were still happy you left, too," she says.

I can't tell if she is embarrassed about that or cool with it, but I guess I don't really care. I start the car and turn around in the road so we can get back to town. Now I kind of wish Sera wasn't spending the night with Chasity because I would really like to spend more time with her alone. She grabs my hand, and we hold them together on top of the console, silently reassuring each other of our feelings, regardless of the crazy night we had at the party.

CHAPTER 10

NOW

I lost weight after the accident, and I wasn't exactly big to begin with. It sucks because I feel like a wimp now. I remind myself that I need to start lifting again. Being blind shouldn't prevent me from being physically fit, and maybe it could help pass the time when I'm not working on homework or sculpting.

My clothes hang on me loosely. I can feel that the button-up shirt I haven't worn in forever is too big, and I don't really have many clothes anyway. I pull it off and throw it towards my bed, deciding to just wear a t-shirt. It's not like I need to impress anyone. Mom organized my drawers to put plain white t-shirts in one drawer with my boxers and socks, and then she put dark colored shirts in one drawer with coordinating shorts, athletic shirts and shorts in another drawer. My jeans hang in the closet, light to dark, followed by khakis and my two button-up shirts. It's very annoying to not know for sure which clothes are which, and trusting my mom to coordinate my clothes feels like I'm five years old. I have always been somewhat sensitive to the way my clothes feel. I hate tags, and if my t-shirts aren't soft, I feel like I'm going to freaking lose it. Weird. I know. But it feels like those issues are even more relevant now. My old t-shirts are comforting even if I probably look like I'm some kind of scumbag who can't afford anything new.

Opting for a tighter fitting t-shirt that I'm pretty sure is the black one I used to wear a lot and some of my faded jeans that are worn with a few holes in them, I throw on my black Docs that I got at a second-hand store several years ago. They were a good deal, twenty bucks for boots I've seen at regular stores for over a hundred. And they are built to last, even when I worked at the shop. I sound like a damn girl all worried about my *outfit*. I'm such a douche. Who really gives a shit what I wear?

My hair is a little longer than I used to wear it. I'm hoping it makes the scar a little less visible, not because I'm vain, but because I don't want the attention. I hate hearing the hushed whispers when people notice me. I can't stay in the background like I used to with my cane front and center, but I can't stand for people to look at me, and even though I obviously can't see them, I can feel it. I can sense the stares, the quiet gasps spoken in my direction. Drives me fucking insane.

Maybe I shouldn't be going out tonight. I'm not sure I'm ready for this. I want to be normal. I want to get out of this box of a house. But this box is comfortable, safe. Confining, but shelter from the shit storm this world seems to rain down on me. Or is this part of the shit, foul, but warm and familiar? Am I sitting right in it?

Ugh.

I'll go. If I can't handle it, I'll just find a way to come back home, to my palace of crap and contentment. To what isn't really life, but existence.

I hear the knock on the door around eight. Mom's at work, so I open the door and am greeted by Ray as he grabs my hand to shake it.

"Dude, it's about time you join the living."

"Whatever, man. Let's go before I change my mind," I say.

"We'll get a couple of beers in ya and see if that'll lighten' you up a little. You sure as hell need it," he says, a smirk evident in his voice.

"Yeah, yeah. And then my blind ass will kick yours in darts."

"Shit. You're not playing darts around me, asshole."

"Hell yeah, I am. Maybe I'll become the next blind dart-playing prodigy," I joke.

I like that I can joke about myself in front of Ray and that he treats me like a normal guy. I'd rather that than have everyone walk on eggshells, always worried about offending me.

Triple Eight is only about fifteen minutes away. We turn into the gravel parking lot and come to a stop. Hearing the car turn off, I tense up a little. Screw it.

"Let's do this." I get out of the car myself and Ray comes around to guide me inside. I decided not to bring my cane. Surely I can get around in a place this size, especially since I plan on sitting in the corner drinking the whole time.

"Aww hell, I can't fucking see," Ray says when we enter. "It's dark in here."

"Welcome to my world, loser," I say, smiling.

"Shut the hell up. Let's go sit back by the pool tables," he says, continuing to lead me.

I find a chair against the wall where I can hear the pool balls clacking to my right. I've been in here a couple of times before and remember that the bar is straight ahead against the opposite wall. Ray heads over to grab us a pitcher of beer. Cigarette smoke fills the room already, and it's not even full yet, just pockets of conversations drifting amid the plumes.

I hear the pitcher of beer plop down on the table and the glasses clank together as they are put down next to it.

Ray pours a drink and slides it towards me so I feel for it quickly, trying not to be too obvious. Downing it, I put my glass back on the table. "Hit me again, dude."

"Sheesh, man. You're gonna be gone too soon if you don't slow it down."

"I can hold my own. Just pour me another."

I sip my next drink, the first one just a good start. Ray is scouting the room for girls, commenting on the hot ones.

"Sexy ass with fine legs, 2 o'clock."

I look in that direction.

"Don't look over there, man. I don't want her to come over here. Gotta see who I like best first," he chides me.

"Seriously? I can't freakin' see, dumbass!"

"Yeah, but you make it obvious when you look in that direction."

"Well, then don't tell me where she is, dipshit."

"I'm just trying to give you a sense of where the hot girls are," he tells me.

"Don't worry about it. I'm not interested."

He just sighs, "Fine. Just drink your beer, but you are not gonna sit here and sulk."

I'm really not interested in some dumb, freakin' hoe in this bar. I had my chance and it's over now. Besides, I don't want a pity screw. And the last thing I need is some girl thinking she can save me. No fucking thank you.

After I've had a few beers and some of Ray's friends are here, I start livening up. A little. Joining in the banter around a pool game, I trash talk with the best of them. I used to be able to kick anyone's ass in pool. I wish I could play, but when Ray sees me feeling sorry for myself, he doesn't let me off that easily.

"Let's see what you got, Cal. Maybe you should put your money where your mouth is."

What the hell? It's not like I can lose anything, and I'm pretty relaxed, my inhibitions gone. Walking to the table that is nearest me on my right, I reach out for a cue stick.

"Hand me the chalk," I say, preparing to see what I can do without sight. Should be interesting. "I'll break."

Ray sets up the balls in the triangle on the table and directs me to the right end while handing me the white, cue ball. I feel around the table so I can set the ball in the middle.

"You better not jack with me, Ray." I hear him laugh.

"Fine. Just a second," I hear him say as he moves the grouping of balls to the center. I had a feeling he would place it to one side. Fucking asshole.

"What? You don't think I'm at enough disadvantage as it is?" I ask, joking back.

"Not from what you've been over there mouthing while the rest of us have played. But it's all good. I could beat you with my eyes closed," Ray says, chuckling.

"You're a fucking dick. Shut the hell up and watch and learn," I say, gathering a little confidence.

I lean over the table and line my cue stick up, excited to participate even though this will be interesting. Sliding the cue stick between my fingers, I shoot the ball directly to the middle hard and hear the familiar sound of the balls breaking. I'm certainly no professional, but I've always enjoyed a good game as well as a little hustling here and there.

I can hear several balls hit the pockets, and obviously Ray has to tell me where the solids and stripes are, but I manage to play a relatively decent match while using his eyes and directions. I really don't give a shit about winning anymore anyway. It just feels so good to be out, experiencing the sounds and smells of life, something I've been missing without realizing it. Ray is a good guy. I'm thankful to have a friend who I can trust. Maybe this is something I will do more often, a little normalcy within reach.

THE NEXT DAY, I ask mom take me to a gym. Now that I don't have physical therapy, I haven't really done enough to stay fit, and after going out last night, I think this will help me. I used to work out all the time at the garage where I worked. They had a pull-up bar and a free-weight set we could use when we weren't busy or after hours.

The gym is at the college. I don't relish the idea of working out alongside other students, but it's free, and I'm not exactly rolling in money. My mom has been trying to get me to talk to a lawyer about the accident because she thinks we could win a case against the man who hit me, but I'm not holding my breath. I've lived without money this long. Quite frankly, I'm not even sure what I would do with extra money anyway. It just reminds me of before.

Apparently Sunday is a busy day at the gym, which is irritating, but there is a guy who works here named Trey who helps me immediately. After giving him my information, he takes me around to tour the room. It is a seemingly large room, but I don't think this gym is huge compared to most. I think I can handle the machine weights and some of the cardio machines without too much help, so Trey leaves me to work on my upper body, telling me to raise my hand when I'm ready to move to another spot so that he can come guide me. I appreciate his willingness to help and especially his giving me the freedom to do this on my own. He acts like I'm not even different, which is cool.

I really love the burn in my muscles as they stretch, pull, and lift, ultimately damaging them so they can grow bigger and stronger. Embracing the pain, I push myself as far as I can go. I strive for the distraction, but my mind still wanders. Counting, working four sets of twenty while increasing the weights each time, I try hard to focus on my breathing. Inhaling, exhaling. But when I think about how it all works, what it takes to reach my goal, I think about my life. I wonder if my life had to be damaged in order to grow. Is there a reason the accident happened to me? That my beautiful light is gone?

Dammit.

There could never be a good enough reason for such a loss. Maybe *I* can grow, learn to cope and even eventually feel something other than the intense pain, but she can't. Her life was taken. Unfair and too soon.

I hate this life without her; a tear quietly escapes but I can't release more. A torrential downpour of emotion dammed inside, building, breaking away and corroding my heart, prevents healing, but I can't allow it to happen yet. Guilt still consumes me and holds my thoughts captive most of the time.

The time passes without my knowledge, and I realize I have completed two exercises each for biceps, triceps, back, chest, and shoulders. Sweat proves my tough workout, but I think my mind was challenged more. My soul continues to search for truth, reason, light in this overwhelming darkness.

I wait with my hand raised just a little because it feels stupid to lift it any higher. I wish there was a better way to get Trey's attention.

"Can I help you?"

The voice, obviously not Trey's, sounds sweet but sort of quiet. I don't answer right away, waiting for confirmation she is talking to me. In a way, I hope she's not because it's embarrassing, but another part of me likes her voice and wants to hear it again. Guilt merges with curiosity.

"Sir, I can help you if you need it. I work here."

Looking in her direction, I feel my lips form a small smile. "Yeah, um, Trey was supposed to come over after I finished my workout."

"Oh, well, Trey had to go on break. I'm sorry." She sounds unsure, and I hate being viewed as fragile, or maybe she just doesn't know how to deal with someone like me.

"No worries. Thanks. Could you just guide me to the locker room? I think I'm done for today," I tell her, thinking I'll have to figure out where my stuff is in the locker room by myself.

"Sure," she says, a smile evident in her voice. She takes my hand and slowly guides me to a door.

I nod at her, silently thanking her, adding, "See ya around." I chuckle at my own joke, but all I hear is her say, "Oh, yeah, no problem. See ya."

And I smile as I feel for my locker having remembered the risen number 49 over it. I'm definitely not looking for a relationship, but maybe having a few more friends would be ok. It's not like I have anything to lose.

BEFORE

Sera is my first girlfriend; that is, she is my first friend who is a girl. Working at the shop with a bunch of guys, I've never really had much opportunity to hang around girls. At school, I sit in the back of most of my classes keeping to myself, getting through it. It's weird because I'm not exactly introverted. I just don't have anything to say to them. They don't interest me. I feel separate from kids my age, like I had to grow up too fast, in some ways at least. Their petty problems are irrelevant. I'm looking ahead. At what? I don't know. But it has to be better than what I've had here.

Until Sera.

After the ordeal at the party, I thought I would be able to continue to stay in my own world at school, but talk crowded me. One of my friends from the shop, Luke, showed me the video of my fight. He thought it was hilarious, but I don't want to think about it. I just want to move on, with my girl. Hopefully, it will die down soon enough, but I don't want our next date to be anywhere where the immature assholes around here could interrupt us.

She jumps on my bike with me after school on a Thursday, and we head to the park where we first hung out. The huge tree waits for us, flowers decorating its roots that sprawl out around the base like octopus legs. This tree has to be a hundred years old, and I wonder what it has endured in its life. What it has seen. It exudes wisdom and strength, a good and beautiful foundation that is a perfect back-drop for our time together.

Even though we have been together for a couple of months, our relationship is still new and fresh. Playful. Sera picks a dandelion and blows it, spreading seed as it's carried into the wind. I notice she closes her eyes before blowing it.

"What did you wish for?" I ask her, enjoying her youthful innocence.

"I can't tell you if I want it to come true," she answers, smiling.

"Hmmm, maybe I could guess then."

She shrugs her shoulders and looks down at the grass where she's sitting. "Maybe..." She looks up at me under her eyelashes and I just want to consume her. She is so incredibly beautiful. But I stifle that thought and continue our banter.

"Ok. I bet you wished for a new puppy."

"Nope, it's way better than that," she laughs, enjoying our little game.

"Ummm, how about a million dollars?"

"Definitely better than that!"

"Must be good then. Hmmmm. I know. You wished for a trip around the world."

"Oooh, that would be awesome, but no. That's not it."

We are sitting with our legs crossed facing each other. She is shy and playful, and I watch her, loving the way her mouth moves when she talks, when she smiles. And the way her eyes communicate what her heart feels. She is lovely and pure. Drawn to her, I raise up on my knees and move towards her.

"Come here," I say quietly, hoping she feels as connected as I do. She moves toward me a little, but seems nervous. I don't know why. We've kissed before. But this moment seems special.

"Closer," I urge. She's playing with me, and it's hot. Tantalizing, she pulls me in, and I slowly take her hand to kiss it. She shudders. I know she feels this too. I lift her chin.

"Look at me." Her eyes meet mine, and I'm lost. In hers.

I lower my head towards hers, kissing her softly on her forehead, her nose, her cheeks, before finally finding her mouth. It's a promise, captivating and moving. And she reciprocates, her hand on my face wrapping around behind my head and bringing me closer. Our bodies are still separate, but our faces touch as we hold each other. It is the most sensual, intense moment, speaking without words what we already mean to each other.

"You guessed it," she says, grinning. I think I've won the lottery because she is definitely my dream come true, everything I could ever wish for. I squeeze her hand, and we sit together until dark, simply enjoying our time together, learning as much as we can about each other, while trying to catch up to our feelings. A few more kisses sprinkled in throughout the sweet evening, the magic remains. In the air, and all around. It becomes a part of who we are and I pray it will sustain me every moment we are apart. I can't wait to graduate so we can live our dreams. Together.

My spirit wants more, and I don't want to drop her off at her house, but it's getting late. The porch light is on when I walk her to her door.

"I can't wait to see you tomorrow," she says, smiling.

"Me, too. I had fun tonight. You mean a lot to me, Sera." I stop myself even though there is so much more I want to tell her. It's too soon. She may be ready to hear it, but it's just not the right time yet. The time will come soon, though, and I can't wait.

I kiss her gently on her gorgeous lips and pull away after only a second when the porch light flickers, apparently her sign to come in. She frowns; "I've got to go... Bye." She lingers a minute before opening the door behind her, slipping in while I silently watch her until the door closes. "Bye, baby," I whisper, touching the door before I retreat back to my bike. And back to my side of the world.

CHAPTER 11

NOW

Because balsa wood is soft, we are carving it for our second sculpture project in art. My last project turned out really well. The texture feels smooth and glossy after Mr. Kenan baked it in the kiln. Very abstract, it's an angel looking up, wings spread wide. The face is smooth, and her posture reflects one who looks towards heaven, illuminating love. I'm pretty sure Mr. Kenan was impressed even if his comments were minimal. Everyone else in the class definitely liked it, offering a lot of praise.

I've continued to keep quiet about my work, though it's nice to hear the admiration among the voices of my peers. Obviously, I can only feel what it looks like, but I think it definitely conveys my theme.

I like carving into the balsa wood because it is easy, but I would choose a harder wood, maybe oak, for future sculptures. I don't want this one to break or become scarred. This class is primarily comprised of beginners, though, so it makes sense to start with something we can all do.

When I reach for my X-Acto knife, Ray chuckles.

"What?" I question him.

"Oh nothing, man. Just thinking it will be fun to watch you sculpt with a freakin' X-Acto knife. I'll keep a first aid kit handy for ya," he teases.

"Always the asshole, aren't you? I'm betting you will need the first aid kit before I will, especially when I throw my X-Acto knife at you. I'll pretend it's the game of darts we didn't get to play."

"Chill out, dude. I'm joking."

"So am I," I say, but continuing to keep a straight face just for fun. My dry sense of humor may entertain me more than it does others.

We had a choice of the size of our carving block, so I picked one that is 6" x 12". I want to create details using imperfect, chunky marks, a "beauty out of chaos" kind of concept. The large wings will fold downward on this one, and her head will be looking down and to the side while she sits on her knees, feet tucked delicately underneath her. The backs of the wings will look as though they are reflecting the light of heaven, or at least I hope I can accomplish what I envision. Thankfully, we have four weeks to finish because I plan to take my time. I have to get it right.

NOT HAVING the ability to drive myself anywhere sucks ass. I hate being cooped up in the apartment. Mom works two jobs so she isn't here half the time, and I don't like asking for help. The bus stops near our apartment, so I've decided to try it for the first time today. I don't have anywhere I have to be, but my mind needs a break. I want to feel fresh air. To feel life, this stagnant apartment suffocating me.

Using the cane is still a challenge. When I had physical therapy, I was taught basic skills, such as holding the cane waist-high and moving only my wrist as I swipe side-to-side in front of my steps. The therapist explained that the wrist is more sensitive to feeling variations on the ground than if I move my arm. They had me try it both ways so that I could feel the difference, which I appreciated because I always want to know *why* about everything. Frustrating that I'll never know *why* this happened to me.

Heading down the stairs from our upstairs apartment has become easier, although I have to hold my cane in my left hand since I hold the railing with my right hand to guide me. The smell of rain saturates the cool air, yet the sound of drops is absent. I can feel the cool prickle of fog hit my face with each step as I walk in this low cloud. It's refreshing and inviting.

I sweep my cane back and forth in front of me while holding my left hand out ahead of my face just in case there is something the cane can't detect. Hopefully, I will become more accustomed to walking alone and navigating the cane relatively soon so that I will at least appear more confident even if I still struggle with the whole overall concept. This is one of those times I am thankful for having had sight prior to the accident. I know the area, the parking lot directly in front of the cold metal and concrete steps that I just descended, and the road with a bus stop straight ahead. It couldn't get much easier than that; at least that's what I'm telling myself as I talk myself through this adventure.

My left wrist adorns a cheap watch that speaks the time for me. It's another convenient and helpful gadget, but I never used to wear a watch so I have to get used to it.

The bus arrives after five minutes. I'm thankful to hear it pull up, the air brakes loud as it comes to a stop in front of me. I don't remember ever noticing people waiting here for a bus before and have even wondered how many people really used it for transportation. Since I had my motorcycle, I guess I took other people's needs for granted in that respect. I sure wouldn't have ever thought I would be sitting here one day boarding a fucking city bus. It's humbling to say the least.

Holding the passport card I received in the mail, the driver comes down to assist me. It's probably obvious I've never done this.

"Hello, sir. Come on up," she says kindly.

Nodding to her, I answer briefly, "Thank you."

"I don't remember having seen you before. I've been driving this bus for five years now. You new in town?" she asks, since I sit on the nearest seat and am apparently in her conversation zone.

"No ma'am. Just new to riding the bus." While I appreciate her help, I don't want to have to explain so I nod my head downward, holding my cane with both hands in between my legs so as not to be in the way. Unfortunately, she is not deterred.

"Where ya headed?"

"Sullivan Park."

"Ahhh, that's a nice park. Older part of town down on the east side. Needs some work, though. I ain't been down in a while, but last time we was there, seemed like things was getting' run down."

"I hadn't noticed," I say, still keeping my responses minimal.

"Oh yeah. I used to take my kids there to play and feed the ducks. Them geese, they don't let the ducks eat. One of 'em chased my son a ways but it didn't take long for that goose to realize my son wasn't gonna take no scarin'. He threw his hands up and started yellin' while chasin' that goose right back on into the water. Funniest thing I ever seen." I nod but before I can even say anything, she's already talking again.

"Yep. Had some good times. So, what you gonna do down there? You meetin' someone?"

"No ma'am."

"You going down there all alone? Boy, you best be careful around all those holes and the water and ere'thing. Ain't no rails 'long that bridge neither," she cautions me.

"Thank you. I'll steer clear of the bridge." I can't help but smile a little at the ridiculousness of the whole scenario. She takes that as encouragement to continue the conversation and I'm wondering how much further it could possibly be. I know it's about fifteen minutes away; surely it's been that long.

"You know, I got a cousin who's blind. My aunt's been taking care of him all his life."

I'm sitting here thinking, *Cool story. Don't know what I'm supposed to say to that.* I sure hope this isn't going to be a common situation. Why do people think I want to talk? Makes me want to say something like, "Oh really? I've got a cousin who drives a bus." Who fucking cares?

Trying to keep my sarcastic responses to myself, I'm very glad when the bus slows and she lets me know we have arrived at the park. Maybe this was all just some sort of weird way of forcing me to move faster because I'm down the two steps and walking away from the bus before she has a chance to give me more advice. I do hear her yell after me, "See you next time. The lake is straight ahead of you." I keep walking and raise my hand up in a small wave. *Sheesh.*

Even though her one-sided banter irritated the hell out of me, I guess I'm glad she oriented me to where I am in relation to the park. Walking forward, my cane leading the way, I tread carefully first on the gravel that turns into bumpy, uneven grass, its cushion allowing my shoes to sink about an inch with each step. I'm not sure exactly where the tree is. I remember the playground was to the left of the parking lot, so Sera and I used to walk in the opposite direction along the water's edge, the map in my mind guiding my current path. The cane reveals a difference when the ground in front of me becomes harder, like packed sand, and I can hear the gentle waves of the small lake, probably agitated by the stormy weather.

The smell of rain surrenders, overtaken by the decay of soggy vegetation and dead fish permeating the immediate air with its stench. No longer a welcome scent. Yet, I retrace my memories as I march toward my past, a place I long to revive.

Finally I feel the lumps beneath the sweeps of my cane before me. The familiar roots accept my visit, as if unaware of my pain. I fall to my knees in reverence and sadness while my tears decorate the skeleton, this web of half-buried tree that I grope, searching for its torso. I know this is our tree, but my fingers find the markings we left bringing assurance and comfort. Grief, self-pity, denial, ache. Dreams, memories, laughter, love.

Cal ~n~ Sera.

The engraving a permanent truth and reminder when memories fade.

Flashes of her smile, her eyes, the sound of her giggle come crashing into my mind, like lightening, the thunder of heartbreak not far behind. It crushes me. It fills me. The reward of torture gratifying.

I sit beneath the tree for what seems like hours before the chill becomes too much, and I remember the last bus won't be much longer. Heading back to the gravelly lot, I wait for reality to set in once more.

BEFORE

The note on my bike feels wrong. Like I already know what it's going to say. Even her writing exposes the tragedy we face. A *Romeo and Juliet* script decided by her father.

Dear Cal,

I have to sneak this note to you. My dad grounded me. I haven't been grounded in forever. I can't believe he's doing this to me! He said he saw my grades online and that I'm apparently too focused on you instead of doing well in school. He took my phone and is picking me up from school every day so now I won't be able to see you as much. I hate this, but I will try really hard to bring my grades up so he won't have any reason to keep us apart. Miss you already...

Love,

Sera

"Dammit!" I hear myself yell while crumpling the paper in my hands. I knew this would happen. I'm not good enough for her, but God, I don't know how to be without her anymore. Smoothing out the paper, I fold it neatly and put it in my back jeans pocket. Once on my bike, I kick the peg back and rev the engine before going to the shop. I can't even haul ass like I want to because it's only a five-minute drive, mostly through residential neighborhoods. But I'm pissed. Hopefully, the old engine I've got on the block will stop these floating images of fear and worry that bombard my mind. *Dammit!*

CHAPTER 12

NOW

"I thought I'd find you in here." Mr. Kenan is talking as he approaches me.

"Yes, sir. Just finishing up my last project."

"I've been wanting to talk to you about your projects," he begins.

"Yeah?" I've gotten good feedback from everyone, including Mr. Kenan, on all of my sculptures, but I haven't really discussed them with anyone. I'm struggling to let them go, to allow them to be seen, because it feels more like I'm revealing everything inside of me. The transparency is so hard. I wanted to create intimate sculptures that reflect emotion. Obviously. But I didn't think about how raw my own emotions still are and how any reflection of me feels like it's through shattered glass. Like my deepest feelings are visible through cracked pieces of a window into my soul, and it's not pretty. My sculptures, band aids, healing the surface of my deepest pain, provide others with the sense of the beauty I have lost. A beauty so profound and rare that it seems unbelievable. Something that can't really be attained. Out of reach. Something taken violently from my desperate grasp.

"You know, Cal, your work is really astounding. To say I'm impressed is an understatement. The whole collection depicts a story, a journey, and I really believe it needs to be shared. This is something real, Cal. Have you considered entering your pieces into the city competition I was telling you about?"

I shake my head, "Nah. I appreciate everything, Mr. Kenan, and I'm glad you like my work, but I don't think it's ready to be put out there like that, or that I'm ready."

"Cal, you've been very tight-lipped about your creations. I know each piece means something more to you than you are willing to tell everyone, but that's the thing about art. You create it, and others not only see the beauty intended, but can find their own feelings associated with it. Your work evokes emotion, meaning that can be transferred, and it's not fair to keep it to yourself. It's not about winning the show. It's more significant than that, Cal."

"Mr. Kenan, do you know what happened to me to cause the loss of my vision?"

"I know you were in an accident. I know you've lost your sight, but what if there was a reason for it? What if it somehow allowed you to create something so compelling and magical that it can be a good thing?"

"Yeah…I lost my sight. It sucks. It does. But my sight is nothing, Mr. Kenan. I lost much more than my sight that day. I lost my light, and that's something I can never get back. My projects obviously can never replace what I've lost, but they are an extension of me. Maybe they are an artificial light, but they are mine, and I can't lose it again."

I hear his sigh of defeat, and of pity.

"I just can't Mr. Kenan," I say again, hoping the conversation is over.

"You have until the end of the week to decide, Cal. Please just think about it a little more. I believe your work needs to be seen. You never know how it might affect others. Don't take from them just because of your own loss. You are stronger than that." His retreating steps, followed by the opening and closing of the lab door, leave me in silence.

Alone, in my darkness. Suspended, rooted in fear. How can I escape? Do I even deserve a reprieve?

Oh God, I need it.

BEFORE

It's been three weeks since I've been able to spend time with Sera, and I'm having withdrawal. I'm on edge. Angry, frustrated, disappointed. Mostly at her dad, but I worry about her feelings being strong enough to outlast the restrictions. She's afraid to disappoint him, but what about me? I want to rescue her, but I'm not sure she wants to be rescued. Secure in the shelter her father veils upon her, she betrays her own emotions, doubting what we have.

The newest note, gingerly placed on my bike, tucked under the edge of the seat, tells me what I don't want to know.

Babe,

My father is right. I need to focus on my grades if I'm going to do well in college. I've been accepted into Baylor, so I will have to leave soon anyway.

I do still care about you, and I hope we can be friends. You make me smile, and I don't want to lose that.

Love,

Sera

You have to be fucking kidding me! What the hell? I can't believe she would just give up on this, on us. I head to the shop even though I don't work today, hoping to forget, to drown out the pain with good ol' alcohol. My go-to in time of need.

Before I take off though, I catch a flicker of light in my peripheral vision and notice Sera watching me from where she is standing next to Chasity's car. She looks solemn, raising her hand to motion goodbye. I can't return the sentiment, though. I refuse to give up, so I shake my head and take off as fast as I can, attempting to leave my emotions behind me, just for a minute. Deferring what I know is true.

ANOTHER WEEK OF MISSED OPPORTUNITIES, and only brief moments of acknowledgment when certainty slips through the filter of indifference, I continually search her eyes for something. Anything. Confirmation of my own feelings reciprocated. But with each small flash of hope comes a blanket of hesitation and doubt, heavy and overcoming any sense of encouragement, stifling my faith and my courage to make things right.

Little moments in passing where our eyes hold each other for a second longer than they should, spur belief, only to be doused each time she withdraws, her eyes first to yield. People surround us in the halls, the cafeteria, oblivious to the battle between us. A contest between love and fear.

CHAPTER 13

NOW

"So Mr. Kenan wants you to enter your work?" Ray asks me. I already know what he's thinking. Ray has been telling me I should make something of my art. He thinks I could turn it into a career.

"How did you find out?" I ask him.

"Everyone in class has been talking about it, Cal. You know your work is good. I don't understand why you want to keep it hidden. I mean, there are a few other projects in class that are pretty good, but yours is different. It's raw. Pure. You've got to do this Cal. Maybe it could lead to more exposure."

"Dude. I don't care about exposure. That's probably the last thing I want, actually. I only do this for me." It's healing. A way to release the pain, the feelings and memories of love and loss. But it's personal, not something to share.

"Come on, man. What's your problem? What are you so afraid of?"

"Shit. Why is everyone so damn insistent? Why do you care?

Huh? What is it to you? It's just a few sculptures. Enter yours if you want to, but don't try to force me to do anything with mine," I say, raising my voice.

"Cal, you need to quit feeling sorry for yourself and freakin' grow some balls. Quit living in your stupid little pity party. You are only hurting yourself," he says, the truth stinging. A hint of repressed tears of anger burn my nose.

"Shut the fuck up. You know nothing about what I've gone through. I can't lose anything because there is nothing left to lose. These sculptures remind me, comfort me, reveal what I had. Reveal something that doesn't need to be understood by anyone but me." I try to rationalize my fear. I created something that surprises me. Even though I can only feel them, my projects exude something so beautiful that I don't want to give it up. It's the closest I can get to feeling even a sliver of what I felt for her.

"Whatever, man. I'm done arguing with you, but I am your friend, and as a friend, you need to know right now that you are being selfish. You are a pretty cool guy, Cal, but you sure can be a dick sometimes."

"Good thing your mom likes dick then, huh?"

I hear him mutter "douchebag" as he walks away, but I know we are still good.

RUNNING on a treadmill can't compare to being outside, but it would be pretty ridiculous at this stage to attempt running outdoors, especially without help. However, running helps me blow off some steam and I need to get back in shape, so I'm at the gym listening to a playlist Sera put together on my iPhone. I was able to retrieve it from the cloud after the accident when I got my new phone. I wish the cloud held more tangible things.

I'm guessing I'm at around a level 7, pushing myself pretty hard when the treadmill slowly stops. Too tired to figure out why it stopped, I carefully step down and bend over putting my hands on my knees after pulling the earbuds from my ears.

"Hi. Sorry to interrupt you." Her voice is familiar, and I recognize her as the girl who showed me to the locker room the first time I came. "You've just been on that thing for over an hour, and I wanted to make sure you don't kill yourself; you know, death by running would be a pretty torturous death." I can hear the smile behind her words, so I smile in kind, hoping she doesn't notice the grimace at the word "death." I don't want to taint everyone I meet just because I'm jaded.

"Hey." I reply, still breathing pretty heavily. "Yeah, that would be a pretty sucky way to go. I guess I let the time get away from me – didn't realize I had been on that long."

"Looked like you were running away from something. I promise nobody was chasing you." I like her feistiness.

"Hmm. You sure about that?" I ask, thinking to myself, what the hell? Might as well open myself up a little.

"Umm, I don't see anyone, so…"

"What about you?" I ask her.

"What *about* me?" she asks, a little attitude reflected in her tone.

"You're here. Are you chasing me?" I say, smiling more broadly now.

"Oooh, aren't *you* movin' right along? And you aren't even running anymore." She chuckles as she continues our little analogy.

"Maybe I'm caught." As soon as it comes out, I feel the guilt trample my senses, and immediately add, "I'm sorry. Never mind. I'm going to go shower. It was good talking to you again," hesitating before I clarify, "I'm sorry; I didn't get your name."

"Emily." Hearing her loss of confidence in her voice, I feel even worse, but I can't do this. I don't think I'm ready. Nobody can replace my light.

BEFORE

I'm hungover as hell. Mom's pissed, says she didn't raise me this way. This isn't learned behavior though. This is my way out. Of my mind. I've been drinking after work every night, but last night the guys and I went to a bar, one where age is overlooked. I had been staying away from this life, from drinking and partying, but anger leads me back. Anger and defiance, against what I can't have, who I can't be. I may as well act the part. If Sera's dad thinks she's too good for me, then why not? I'll be who I can be. I don't give a shit.

It's Friday and there is no chance I'm going to school, even after Mom yelled at me and tried to drag me out of bed.

"Get. Up!" she yells at me. I assume she's already tried to wake me several times. I continue to ignore her. Preferring quiet.

"Damn it, Cal! Get your ass up for school! You know I don't like you drinking and staying out late, but if you quit going to school, what will you do? Work in a gas station forever? Oh, that's great. You want to be like me? Huh? Wanna take after your old mom? Working 'til you can't keep your eyes open just to make ends meet? Answer me!"

I don't think she took a breath the whole time she was yelling at me. I hold my pillow over my head and just grunt a muffled response, "Ok. Ok, just chill. I'm just staying home one day. It'll be fine."

"One day too many, Cal. You've got to get a hold of yourself before it's too late. Ugh. I'm so tired of this. I try to do my best by you but this...this is just a waste. A waste, Cal. You better be up when I get home. If you can't go to school, then you should at least be able to clean yourself up and get some work done around the house. Your room smells disgusting."

At that, she leaves. I don't even care that she got in the last word, as long as it *was* the last word. I could do without hearing any loud noises of any kind for the rest of the day. Closing my eyes, I drift back to a heavy sleep, eluding school, Mom, life.

And I won't even allow myself to think about Sera.

CHAPTER 14

NOW

With the Fall semester winding down, and a couple more days until Mr. Kenan is taking the various projects to the city show, I decide to have Mom help me to pick up my work.

I've gotten pretty good at getting around the parts of campus I use without help, so it bothers me to need help, especially from my mom. I love her and I appreciate her, but it's still embarrassing. Nobody will say anything because they probably feel sorry for me, which sucks even more.

"Mom, you don't need to lead me right now. I know my way."

"I'm sorry, hon. I was just trying to help." I can hear the hurt in her voice. Her sensitivity frustrates me because obviously I'm not just going to be an asshole to her, but God, I'm 19 now, having had the most *joyful* birthday ever back in the summer when I was in rehab.

I remember the nurses sang to me. It was bleak, really. I insisted they keep it minimal, not feeling a desire to celebrate anything at all.

Mom can't stand a moment without conversation. "So, I can't wait to see the projects you have been working on. You haven't mentioned much about them until now, but you obviously did a lot of work since I need to help you to get them home."

"Thanks for the reminder, Mom," I reply sarcastically. Maybe I can't help being an asshole.

"Cal, you know I don't mean anything by that. I'm just happy to get to see your school and what all you have been doing."

"Mom, seriously, this is college. Please don't embarrass me in there."

"Fine. You are so sensitive. Can't I just be a proud Momma for a little while? Gosh," she says, talking more to herself as she continues to rattle on. And she thinks *I'm* sensitive? I give up.

I always relished the cool breeze as I entered the double doors to the art department during the hotter months, but today it's pretty cold, so the warmth of the building felt as soon as we enter is nice and soothing. The cold weather is a changed concept for me. I've heard people say it makes old injuries hurt, but I always thought they were full of crap, or just old or something. But my legs and arms are aching more and more lately, and the cold seems to make it much worse.

The accident didn't just take my sight. Along with several skull fractures, a broken right leg and arm, as well as a hairline fracture to my hip, I was actually placed in an induced coma for a week. I don't remember that part of course, but I guess it all contributes to the difficulties I deal with now, and will probably have to manage for the rest of my life. I was so focused on losing Sera that my physical pain was, in a weird way, a welcome distraction.

The art building is several stories high not including the basement, but the lab is thankfully on the first floor. I turn right just after entering and Mom starts in again.

"Oooh, this is nice, Cal. Hold on. Do you have any of your work on display in these cases?"

"Well, I can't exactly see what's in the cases, Mom, but considering I told Mr. Kenan that I'm not interested in showing my work, I highly doubt it."

"Cal! I'm sure your projects are good enough to be in here. Why would you do that? You don't give yourself enough credit, you know? Good grief. I know my kid deserves to have his work put on display. I mean, he's handsome and smart and very talented. Why wouldn't they just put it in there anyway?"

I think she's still talking, but I've turned her off. She seems to think we are at pre-k open house.

Continuing to walk without her, I hear Mom's feet shuffling quickly behind me to catch up. I want to make this quick. The lab has become a home away from home for me, almost a place where I can be someone else, create something better than my circumstances. I wasn't expecting anyone to be around today, so I'm surprised to hear Mr. Kenan talking to Ray from the opposite side of the room. They quieten when I near them, obviously making me a little suspicious, but I remind myself that everything isn't about me. Maybe Ray needs help or something.

I walk towards their voices, sticking my hand out to shake Ray's. "What's up, dude?"

"Not much. Just leaving," he replies on his way out.

When I shake Mr. Kenan's hand, he puts his other arm on my shoulder. "Hello, sir. I just came to pick up my things before break."

"Well, I'm glad you came by, Cal. Why don't we sit down and talk for a minute since you are here?" Before I can ask him more, I hear Mom coming in the door.

"Cal, why didn't you wait for me? I was trying to tell you something. I did see your work in the case. It's beautiful, son. Why didn't you tell me you are so creative?"

"What?" Surely I didn't hear that correctly. I've kept my work together in my lab space.

"Mr. Kenan? This is my mom, Trish. Please show her where I keep my work. I think she must be mistaken."

"Son," he addresses me carefully.

"Mr. Kenan, I am not your son. Please don't patronize me. Did you put my work on display without asking me? You know I don't want that."

"Cal, I didn't enter your work in the city competition. Yet. I still hope you will reconsider. But you didn't say I couldn't display it in the commons. It helps other art students to view various work. Everyone learns from each other; that's part of the growth of an artist, Cal."

"Really?" I ask sarcastically, continuing, "Because I am not looking at everyone else's work, Mr. Kenan. Are you saying I can't grow as an artist because I can't see to learn?" I know that's not what he's saying, but I'm pissed. This work is mine.

My mom, of course, intervenes, "Cal, I'm sure Mr. Kenan does not mean that at all, and you know it. You stop being ugly and be thankful he recognizes your talent. There is no reason to be like this."

Mr. Kenan addresses my mom, "I'm sorry, Ma'am. Cal has expressed his feelings about keeping his work private with me. And I understand your frustration"; he turns toward me, "but sometimes it takes that extra push to help a person out of one's comfort zone. What would happen if we didn't have Michelangelo, Monet, or Van Gogh? They each had challenges. Many artists' works are rejected or the artists don't feel their work is complete or good enough, but if they choose to never allow their work to be seen, not only would we not be able to learn from it, but we would have little to appreciate and enjoy. Cal, your work is bigger than you. It is worth being seen."

It hurts to put myself out there like this. My work reflects my emotions, my pain, my inspiration, my love, all things I am afraid to share. I feel like I have to hold on tight or I will have nothing left of me.

"Mr. Kenan, I understand what you are saying, but my work is sacred to me; it's all I have that keeps me sane," I tell him, exposing more of my fear than I want to.

"I get that, Cal. I really do. But you know, everything you have endured can become your testimony, expressed through art. It can help others as they interpret your work in their own way. If nothing more, it is inspiring and uplifting. Don't allow your fear to make you selfish. Just take that step; I believe it will actually free you from some of the pain and repression, not only helping you, but blessing others at the same time," Mr. Kenan says, thoughtfully.

Nodding my head in defeat, I finally give up. "Ok. Do it. Enter all of it in whatever competitions you want. But don't expect me to be there. I don't even want my name on it. Can you at least give me that?"

Mr. Kenan sighs, but concedes. "That's fine, Cal. I can do that. I think this is a big step for you, and an important one. Believe in yourself, Cal. God has given you a gift, one that should be shared."

"God took my ability to see, Mr. Kenan. Do you think he gave me this gift to placate me? Because nothing can make it better."

"You already had this gift, Cal. Now you have the opportunity to use it. Move forward. You have to live now. I'm sorry for what happened to you, and I don't believe God took your sight, but either way, you can't continue to let that define you. Just like you mold clay, you are also being molded, every day by the choices you make, by your relationships, by who you are, but if you try to prevent it, you will be stunted. Let yourself be molded into something great, because everything in this life can contribute to making you better, as long as you allow it."

"It's just hard, Mr. Kenan. Really hard."

Mom has been quiet, which surprises me. I expected her to join Mr. Kenan in his lecture. I haven't heard her get up and leave, so I assume she's still standing with us.

"Mom? Let's go."

"Ok, hon," she replies, grabbing my arm lightly to lead me out.

I shake her off, still frustrated, and hear her sigh.

"I'm sorry," I spit out harshly, but I quickly try to soften my tone to let her know it's not her. "I'm sorry..."

"It's ok, Cal. Let's just go."

This time, she doesn't touch me; in fact, I hear her walk away quickly, the door opening and closing before I can even get to it.

"See you soon, Cal." I hear Mr. Kenan say as I'm leaving.

I lift my hand to wave in response, feeling a little defeated, but also a bit nervous and maybe excited in anticipation of my future. A future potentially illuminated with belief. In something more than myself.

BEFORE

A month left of school. I can do this, I think, after spending the entire weekend self-medicated, alcohol dimming anything and everything in my mind.

Monday's are shit. Getting up early for school is shit. But I can do anything for just one month, and then I'm out. Out of this hell-hole of futile, fucking shit.

Anger masks my hurt, cloaking my feelings with cynicism. Who cares, though? Right? I mean, Mom's at work. She's sick of my attitude and hasn't been talking to me anyway. I never talk to anyone at school, so I say *fuck it*. I'll get through my last month of school and never look back.

The pep talk in my head challenges me to get dressed, drive to school, park my bike, head up the stairs, and force myself into school, the institution of conventionalism. Everyone is here to achieve the same goal. To finish. To get to the next step.

"What are your plans for after high school?" I remember Sera's dad asking me. And I think, how the hell am I supposed to know? I'm only 18 years old, not ready to be a boring grown up. Why does that make me less than anyone, especially him?

Walking with my head down, my jaded and negative thoughts prevent me from noticing where I'm going in the hall before I have run into someone hard. Dammit.

"I'm sorry." I mutter, trying to pick up the person's belongings off of the floor. I'm trying to hurry because per usual, I'm barely going to make the bell. I don't even notice her scent. I can't hear what she's saying to me. My mind is protecting me, keeping me in a weird cloud of oblivion. It's not until her hand is on mine, stopping it from stacking books and papers, that I feel Sera's presence and hear her sweet voice speaking my name calmly.

"Cal. Cal, stop."

I freeze. Maybe I can just stay in this moment and pretend all is ok. Her hand is still on mine and it feels nice. Right.

After a long moment of hesitation, my eyes lift to see hers, watery, searching mine for what's wrong. Her tears devastate me, but my anger prevails.

I lift my hands up, surrendering, the martyr in me speaking loud and clear. "Fine. If you don't need my help, I'll be going."

I don't want to leave. I really don't want to punish her, but I'm just so mad. Frustrated. Exasperated.

Shaking my head, I sigh. "Sorry," I quietly say, not making eye contact.

"It's ok," she replies, softly. Clearly hurt. "It has to be ok, Cal."

My eyes question hers. I truly don't know what she's thinking. I want to grab her and hold her in my arms forever, and it's taking everything in me to move. My feet take me backward, maintaining this superficial hold, eye to eye, until I can bear it no more, and I turn to walk away.

I HAVEN'T SEEN Sera at lunch, at the door where we leave every day, or in the halls for the last week. Seeing her this morning has changed my day. It has changed me. Determined insurgency arouses my spirit. I don't know why I allowed doubt or fear to envelop me. It's not who I am. And it damn well isn't going to stop me from getting what I want ever again.

I don't know how Sera has been leaving school without my seeing her this past week, so I decide to leave my last class early. The substitute teacher sitting at the desk in the front of the room is indifferent anyway.

Waiting and watching other seniors leave, I patiently stand out of sight when the door opens once again. She exits with her head down, so she startles when I grab her wrist, swinging her around close to me.

"Sera, It's ok. It's just me," I quietly tell her.

"Cal, what are you doing? My father will see us. He's been picking me up, himself."

"I don't care anymore, Sera. Tell me you don't want me. That you don't want us."

She lifts her eyes, slowly, but assuredly. "Cal. I can't. It's not about what I want."

"Yes it is, Sera. Don't you see? We are 18. We don't have to do what anyone tells us to do. This is our life, and our choice," I argue. "Please, Sera. This last couple of weeks has been hell. I haven't been myself without you."

"I haven't either, Cal. I've missed you so much. You move me, and you know I've been stuck for a really long time."

My hand raises to gently wipe the tears trailing down her smooth cheeks. "Babe. I feel something with you. You mean so much to me. Please. We can figure this out. We have to."

Sera glances out at parking lot and grabs my hand, dragging us back inside.

"What are you doing?" I ask.

"My dad isn't here yet. I don't want him to know I've been talking to you. I'm sorry. It's just...easier that way."

"I don't care about that," I say, trying to reassure her.

"Ok. So, how are we going to do this? We don't have much time before I have to leave to go to college. How will we stay together then?"

"Let's just get through right now. Meet me tomorrow after school. See if you can get out early and meet me here. I'll try to come up with a plan. Ok? Just, don't stress," I say, drawing her close to me. It feels so good to hold her. Her hands hold me tight, wrapped around my back as I kiss the top of her head, one hand around her waist, the other stroking her hair.

"You have no idea how good it feels to hold you again. I'm sorry about this morning, by the way. I've just felt so angry. But after seeing you, I knew I couldn't stay away anymore. I really believe we are meant to be together, Sera."

"Oh my gosh, Cal. I feel the same way. Just... don't leave me. Ok? Please don't ever leave me."

"I won't, babe. Not ever," I whisper into her hair.

We both notice a car pulling up to wait by the stairs so we quickly break apart. Sera looks at me as she grabs my hand, holding it until she can't anymore, and walks out the door.

CHAPTER 15

NOW

Christmas break. I never thought I would wish I was in school, but since I don't have a job, the mundane and thoughtless acts of habit smother me. Without a place to be, my apartment stifles me, even music becoming redundant. I don't have supplies to work on sculpting, and the lab is closed for the holidays. I have gone to the gym a few times, but it's desolate considering most students have gone home to be with their families during the holidays.

Mom is still working two jobs, at the factory during the day and at a sandwich shop on weekends and some nights. I wish I could help out somehow.

Every little step in full recovery is like a giant leap for me. School, the gym, my art, all of it demands courage that is still growing from a tiny seed inside of me. My therapist quotes the bible, "if you have faith as small as a mustard seed, you can say to this mountain, 'Move from here to there,' and it will move. Nothing will be impossible for you."

"And what if I don't?" I question him with uncertainty.

"Do you know how big a mustard seed is, Cal? It's about 1 to 2 millimeters. A tiny piece of grain. Picture a mark of a pen on your finger. Do you have that much faith, Cal?"

It's perplexing. I honestly don't know how much faith I have, or if I have any at all. And I don't know what, or who, to have faith in.

"In myself?" I ask, feeling unenlightened.

"In yourself, yes, but ultimately in God, Cal," he answers.

"I don't really know, I guess. I've not given *God* much thought." I wasn't raised in church. Mom rarely talked about it. On special occasions, she would pray over a meal or something like that, but I didn't know a whole lot about religion.

"That's ok. It's not too late to think about God. But what I'm trying to say to you right now is, I believe God is our creator. He protects us and helps us along the way of life. We don't have to be alone or do things without His help, and if you have a tiny inkling of faith in Him and His ability to help you, He will take care of the rest. It's ok to lean on God."

"Ok. Umm, I guess I have a 'tiny inkling of faith,'" I say, sort of mocking his mini sermon. I didn't realize therapists could express their religious views to patients. I'm not sure how I feel about it. I mean, I do believe in God, but I don't really know much about Him. I didn't even know that the *faith as big as a mustard seed* saying was from the bible, having not really contemplated it before anyway.

"You can do what you want in life, Cal. Don't let fear cause you to stumble," Dr. Roberts continues.

"It's not like I'm trying to. It's hard, though...being blind. It sucks. I miss seeing. Colors, the sky, trees, my mom, my..."

I can't. I miss her so much; it hurts deep in my soul. I keep on moving, distracting myself with school and art and friends, but she's always there in the back of my mind. I constantly hear her whispering my name, "Cal." Like she's trying to reach me. I don't believe in ghosts. It's not like that. But in my head, she's there, haunting my present with my past. Not in a bad way, but it doesn't make living my life now any easier. I don't want to discuss Sera with Dr.

Roberts, though. Not now and maybe not ever. I just have to move on.

I can hear him breathing, waiting for me to continue. "I know. I shouldn't feel sorry for myself. I have to pick myself up and start over. Ugh. It really does suck, though, for lack of a better way to say it."

With a smile in his voice, he replies, "It's fine, Cal. You are feeling *something*. That's better than nothing, and the fact that you recognize that 'it sucks' means that you want better. You have something to reach for even if you don't know exactly what it is yet. Just keep going forward. You are capable, and when you don't feel like you are, say a little prayer. God is able."

Again with the God stuff, I think. I don't know why it's bugging me; it's not like I'm offended. I think I just feel inferior, or ignorant, and I hate that. And if I'm honest with myself, I'm angry at God. I don't understand why I had to go through everything I've gone through. It's not fair. The common phrase, "life isn't fair," comes to mind. What a fucking understatement.

WE BOUGHT our first real Christmas tree this year. Mom thought since I couldn't see the decorations, that maybe I could smell them. It was really thoughtful. I do love the smell of pine. Bringing a little nature inside the house adds a freshness to our tiny apartment. It cleanses and adds beauty to the colorless world surrounding me.

I sculpted a rose out of clay for my Mom when I had some extra time before the art lab closed. I knew I wouldn't be able to buy her a Christmas present this year, so hopefully she will like it. Wrapped in newspaper, it sits under the tree with one other present, something I assume she plans to give me.

Christmas has never been a huge thing at our house, considering it's just the two of us, but this year somehow seems a little more special to me. I realize that with everything I've lost, that *I'm* still here. My mom has told me multiple times that she is grateful that I'm still alive after such a horrific accident, but I've never been able to consider that as *good* until now. I'm finally recognizing a little of my worth, if nothing else, to her. My mom would have been alone had I not made it, and just thinking about her grief makes me understand her clinginess.

I decide to include a card, really just a piece of folded piece of paper. I write, "I love you, Mom. I'm thankful for you (even if you do drive me a little nuts sometimes – haha)."

Smiling, I attach it to the present. Things have been way too serious for way too long. It's time to lighten the mood. I'm making that my early New Year's Resolution, to lighten up and to have a little more faith.

The door creaks as it opens, inviting a frigid wind as Mom breezes in, singing her words, "Merry Christmas Eve, Cal! I have tomorrow off. Isn't that great?" She's clearly very cheery.

"Merry Christmas Eve to you too, Mom. That *is* great. You deserve a break," I say, smiling as I greet her.

"Thank you, Cal, but you know it's just what I've got to do. I would never trade my life as your Mom."

She's told me this a million times. I just nod and tell her, "I know, Mom. Thank you."

She asks, "So, do you want to open your present tonight or wait until tomorrow? I really want to give it to you now." She's always enjoyed giving me things even if she can't do it very often, and she always has a hard time keeping it a secret.

I chuckle. "Sure; let's open them tonight." I'm anxious to give her mine, too, so I reach under the tree, grab the card and present, and hand them to her.

"Cal, when did you...?" I can hear tears mark her voice.

"It's nothing, Mom. I just made a little something for you at school."

She reads the card out loud (which I hate), but I gladly hug her back when she grabs me.

"I love you, son. I know I don't say it much, but I do. I don't love your attitude when you are feeling angry, but I will be here for you no matter what. I hope you always remember that."

"Thanks, Mom. Now quit your crying and open the present," I say, teasingly.

"Ok, ok." I can hear the paper ripping and wish I could see her face when I hear her gasp.

"This is so incredibly beautiful. I cannot believe you made this. I mean, I can, but gosh, Cal, do you even know how gifted you are? I love this."

"Thanks, Mom. I'm sure it could be better. I was just thinking, 'I've never given you flowers....'"

"It's perfect. Thank you so much, dear," she says, understanding my modest shrug.

I hear her clap her hands with excitement. "Ok. Now you have to open yours. Hold on." She doesn't go to the tree, but outside.

"Where are you going?" I ask.

"Just a second," she yells while running away from the apartment.

What the heck? I have no idea what she's doing. She doesn't even have to blindfold me for effect, I think, grinning.

I've moved closer to the door when I hear it swoosh open again with the cold wind, but I'm more focused on listening for any clues as to what in the world Mom is bringing in. I hear breathing. No. It's more like snorting.

"Cal, meet Luke," she says, placing a leash in my hand. I can't believe it. She mentioned once that I should get a service dog, but I know how hard it is to get a trained dog, as well as expensive.

"This is freakin' awesome, Mom. Where did you get him? Describe him to me," I say, immediately squatting and feeling his head. He is sitting at my feet, very calmly, but licks my face happily.

"He's a yellow lab, about 70 pounds. He's 16 months old and recently graduated from a training program where they train guide dogs for the blind. I inquired online and they shipped him here from Oregon on an airplane, sooo, I picked him up just now. He's beautiful. I think he will be a great addition to our little family. What do you think?"

I can't stop smiling as I hug and pet him. "Hi, Luke. You're a good boy, aren't you? Yes you are."

Then I remember the other present under the tree. "Then what's under the tree?" I ask Mom.

"Oh yeah. Let me get it. It's for Luke." I guide Luke a few steps to the living room and sit down on the edge of my recliner so that I can continue to pet him.

"Here you go, Luke," she says, unwrapping and handing him a toy. "Hold on. We have to take your harness off, huh?" Mom explains to me that when he has his harness on, he is working, but when it's off, he can play.

"Apparently they normally insist that you spend time with him in the facility where they train him and won't let him go home with you for a couple of weeks, but they were really kind and have arranged for someone local to help you learn how to use him," she informs me.

"Huh. I just can't believe you were able to get him. Wasn't he too much?" She knows I understand we don't have much money.

"Well, actually, I applied for a special grant and we were approved. I think God has been looking out for us."

Hmm. She never talks like that, but after what Dr. Roberts said, I'm starting to wonder. Maybe God really is helping us when we need it.

Now that his harness is off, Luke playfully puts his paw on my leg.

"What is it, little fellow?" It's like he's hitting me, trying to get my attention.

Mom says, "Maybe he wants you to play fetch with him?"

Chuckling, I toss the toy toward the bathroom at the end of our short hallway. "Go get it!"

Luke takes off and is back within seconds, holding the toy at my knees. It becomes quite slobbery after several fetches, but I'm so happy to have him that it doesn't matter to me at all.

"I really love him, Mom. Thank you so much," I say, to which she quietly replies, "of course, son."

After dinner, we head to bed, Luke by my side.

Yeah, I think things are going to start getting better.

BEFORE

I lie awake in my bed thinking about Sera and what I want to say to her tomorrow after school. What I need to say to her.

Her dad is being a dick. I know he wants good things for his daughter, and he obviously doesn't consider me as "good." She makes me good, though. I mean, what the hell? Money doesn't make people good, and lack of money doesn't make people bad. It just irritates the hell out of me that he judges me without even knowing me.

I can't sleep. It's hot in my room. I decide to write Sera a note. Maybe then I can get all of my thoughts out at once.

Sera ~

God, there's so much I want to say to you. I've been lying in my bed thinking about us. I know your dad doesn't think I'm good enough for you. I really want to be, though. You make me more than I am. I feel like I'm on the top of the world, like I'm fucking Superman, when I'm with you. But I don't want to drain you. I want to make you feel that way, too. I want to be the one who lifts you higher, compliments who you are, brings out your best. And I don't know exactly how to do that, Sera. But I do know that I desire your happiness above all things. I will do everything in my power to always be there for you. If you want to go to school, I will support you. If you want to go explore the world, I will be by your side. I just can't *not* be with you. Because when I'm not with you, I'm not me. I feel like we are supposed to be together. I really do believe that what we have is real. I know we are young. It's not like I'm trying to get married and have kids and whatever else. I just want to grow with you. I want to learn with you, experience life and everything in it, with you. Only with you.

Please take this journey with me. Please stay with me, go with me, do life with me. Because I pretty much can't do it without you.

So, hopefully I am convincing you, because I'm ready to take this on. You and your sexy self, and me- we are good. And we deserve good.

So, yeah, let's do this. Now maybe I can freaking go to sleep. If nothing else, do it for my sleep's sake. Haha

Ok, I'm rambling now...

With all my love (and everything that comes with it),

~Cal

THE HOURS of this day have seemed like years as I wait to finally meet with my beautiful girl. My Sera. My light. Distracted in all of my classes, I have somehow made it through the day on autopilot because I don't remember learning anything. Of course, half the time, I don't know how much I'm really learning in this stupid school anyway. Fucking high school. It's a waiting game.

With the school day finally behind me, I walk to my favorite double doors, made beautiful by her. I think the only great thing about this school is that nobody really cares that she and I are meeting before school is out. No questions, no weird looks from teachers. Thank God. It's currently the only safe place we can be together freely.

Straight, smooth hair that I have come to know so well is all I can see from where she waits behind the small entryway, and already, electricity runs through my veins. I'm smiling like a big idiot, but I feel like I could fly, or jump the length of the hall just to reach her. Then I chuckle when another student passes me in the hall muttering, "What the fuck are you smiling at?" I'm sure I look like a dumbass to him. I was *that guy* just yesterday.

And then I'm with her, my left hand grabbing her left arm, my right curling around her waist pulling her close to me, breathing her in.

I slipped my note to her early in the day through a guy I know who is an office aid first period. I knew he would be able to get it to her. He works with me at the shop so I trusted him not to read it. Plus, I put it in a sealed envelope to make it look more important so the teacher would let her have it.

"Did you get my note?" I ask her, feeling content and complete with her in my arms.

"Yes." She pulls away so that she can see my face, and her teary smile says so much.

"God, babe. You are so fucking beautiful." It's ridiculous how soft I've become but it's worth it. "Well...?" I prod, needing to hear her response.

"I got it, and you don't have to convince me. I want to be with you, too. You know, Dad just wants me to go to school, grow up some before getting into a serious relationship. It's been my goal forever, too. Since I was a little girl, I just wanted to make him proud, and I still hate the idea of letting him down."

I start to interrupt her, worrying this isn't going the way I want it to, but she touches my lips, "Shhh, let me finish."

"Ok," I say quietly, silently praying to God, or whoever is in charge of the universe, to please be on my side. *Please let me have a chance with her.*

"So, as I was saying..." she says, smiling, "I don't want him to be disappointed in me, but maybe we can somehow get through to him. The thing is, I know you want to leave and not go to college yet. That idea scares me so much, but it also thrills me. I've been thinking a lot about it."

"Babe, we don't have to do that. I just want to be with you," I say, assuring her we can work it out.

"I know, Cal. I'm not saying that. You've actually never even asked me to go with you, so I know you aren't trying to change my path. But, like I said, I've been thinking about it, and even though it freaks me out, I kind of want to do that, too, like, before I go to college. I could still go to college. I just...I don't know what I want to be. I'm not ready to decide my life right now. I think travelling, experiencing life with you for maybe a year or so, God, that sounds amazing to me. But you know my father will die. There's no way he's gonna let it happen, so I haven't exactly figured that part out yet. But, yeah...I want nothing more in this world than to be with you," she concludes, beaming up at me, surely knowing what her words mean to me.

Before I can even talk I'm hugging her so tight. "Let's get out of here. Please tell me you can leave with me. We really need more time, like, right freaking now." I smile at her. She is my everything.

"Actually..." she says in a teasing tone, "I kind of told my dad that I was going home with Chasity after school to study. He asked a lot of questions, which is annoying because he doesn't trust me, although maybe he's right not to, but anyway, I think he finally believed me. Especially after he talked to the *cougar* and she vouched for me," she says, giggling.

"Hmmmm, maybe the cougar isn't horrible after all. But I think I'll still keep a safe distance from her," I say, laughing with her.

"Soooo, do you wanna hang out here in the school all day or what?" She's in a silly mood.

"Hell no! I need a little more privacy for what I'm going to have to do to get you back for keeping me in suspense," I say, nudging her side.

She yelps and takes off running. "You have to catch me first."

And Oh God. This silly version of Sera is fucking stunning.

I walk quickly behind her, just enjoying the moment, before jogging to catch her just as she reaches my bike. I can't wait any-fuck-ing-more. I'm kissing her with all I have, making up for each lost moment, and promising a love I haven't been able to speak with words yet but that I'm realizing is consuming me.

CHAPTER 16

NOW

I've had Luke for two weeks, and Shannon, the trainer who worked with us, finally gave me a certificate of completion for the initial training period. Apparently, there is a support group and other classes and events I can attend if I want to travel thirty miles, but I'm thinking I'm not interested. I didn't tell Shannon that. She was very nice, but a little overenthusiastic if you ask me. She won't take *no* for an answer, and I don't feel like arguing with her.

I never really thought about how much work it is to have a dog in general. Taking him out for walks and grooming him, keeping him up-to-date on health care, it's all a big responsibility, and it takes me out of my comfort zone. I'm not able to sit inside all day. And when we are out, Luke takes his sweet time locating the perfect spot to relieve himself.

It's weird because this last month of not being in school, while it started out boring, has kind of caused me to revert back to my introverted self, and I feel nervous about starting back on Monday. Mom said she already contacted the school regarding Luke, but I'm a little concerned that he will bring unwanted attention. Like I'm not already obvious enough.

~

GRUNTS, the clank of weights, and the swooshing of the treadmills reveal all of the students are back in full force. I debated bringing Luke with me today to the gym. Would he get in the way? Of me, or of others? I decided, though, that it would be a good way for me to reintroduce myself to school life but with Luke by my side, so here we are, standing outside the dressing room against the wall while I listen and work out in my mind where there might be an open spot on machine weights.

I'm feeling out of my element.

Just before I decide to turn back and head home, I hear a familiar voice.

"Oh my gosh! Cal! He's so cute. What's his name?"

"Emily?"

"Yes, it's me. So what's your dog's name? I just love him!"

"Oh, umm, yeah, his name is Luke. Actually, I'm not supposed to let people pet him or anything while he is working. Sorry." I feel like an ass. I don't want to be rude, but I'm not sure how else to say it. Shannon was adamant that I don't allow people to distract Luke, especially since he's still pretty new at this, too.

She sounds embarrassed. "Oh. I'm sorry. Well, do you need help with anything today?" Back to business.

"It's all good. I just got him and we are both still learning. But, yeah, I was just thinking maybe it's too crowded for me today. What do you think? Are all of the machines being used?"

"Well, actually, there's one over in the corner. Come on. I'll take you." I can tell she's unsure about how to go about directing me, so I reach my hand out and tell her, "Lead the way. I'll lead Luke." In training, I learned that guide dogs don't lead the blind, but rather, the owner leads the dog. Dogs don't know the way to go unless we command them, but they are able to warn the owner of bumps, holes, or obstacles.

She grabs my hand and it feels warm. I squeeze it a little. I justify it in mind that I'm just trying to show her that I'm thankful for her help, but deep down, I recognize I'm longing for touch, for attention. Pushing back my conflicted feelings, I push forward, continuing to pursue something more with this girl.

It takes less than a minute for all of these thoughts to run through my mind before we are already at the machine and she's letting go of my hand.

"Here we are. You can let Luke sit right over here while you work out. It's great seeing you, Cal. I'll be around helping other people, but just wave your hand when you're ready and I'll come back. Ok?"

"Ok, thanks." I smile in her direction. I probably pissed her off when I told her she couldn't pet Luke, but I'm hoping she can get past that. My lack of confidence irritates me. I was never *overconfi-*dent, but God, now I feel like such a loser sometimes.

After about 45 minutes of working out my lower body, I wave my hand. Damn, I hate looking like such an idiot. Honestly, I could get back to the locker room without help now, but I'm hoping for one more chance to talk to Emily before I leave.

She is there quickly, saying, "Hey, Cal. All done?"

"Yep. So, how much longer do you have to work today?" I ask, feeling brave.

"Oh, umm, actually, I leave in five minutes. Why? What's up?"

"Well, I was just wondering if you might want to get a drink or something. I'll let you pet Luke." I tease her.

Her giggle is cute. The sparks I had with Sera are not there, but I figure that was a one-time thing anyway. And I'm not looking for a girlfriend. I just want a little companionship.

"Sure. Sounds fun. I'll meet you outside in, like, five minutes. Is that ok?" she asks. I guess she's not overconfident either.

Smiling, I nod my head before going to change clothes. "Good boy, Luke. Come on; let's go," I say, grabbing his harness. Maybe he is good for more than one thing, I think, chuckling.

∼

"Sorry it took me a minute. I had to help Trey unlock some lockers before I could leave. So where do you want to go?" I hear her say, as soon as she exits the building. I was starting to wonder if she'd changed her mind.

"No problem. How about the Commons? We can sit where those couches are."

"Ok."

This time I just start walking in that direction since I know my way. It's only about a five-minute walk since the campus is pretty small.

After we grab a couple of cokes, we sit down on some couches that are a little more secluded than the rest. I can still hear a lot of chatter around me considering classes resume tomorrow, but at least here, we can hear each other better.

"Thanks for joining me," I tell her.

"Of course. I'm glad you asked."

Our conversation is a little awkward. Neither of us knows what to say, so I finally decide to just try to get to know her better.

"So, what's your major? Are you from here?"

"English, and yes. How about you?"

"Art and also yes. Seems like we should already know each other then."

"Umm, yeah, I kind of do know you, Cal. Maybe you would recognize me if...nevermind. But yeah, I was in a couple of classes with you last year."

"Oh. Shit. I'm sorry. I didn't really talk to many people in high school. Kind of did my own thing."

"It's ok. I have always been pretty shy. Plus, you had a girlfriend anyway, right?"

"Yeah. I guess you would know all about my situation then, huh? Everyone knows everything around here." It bugs the hell out of me. I hate everyone knowing my story, or at least thinking that they do. "We can just not talk about that, though. K?"

"Of course. Sorry."

Back to awkward silence.

I'm doubting this whole thing. It's too soon. I don't know what the hell I was thinking.

I can hear Emily shift in her chair.

"I'm sorry," I say. "I don't mean to sound like a jerk. It's just...still kind of hard for me. Ya know? I mean, obviously, the wreck changed everything for me, so yeah..."

"It's ok. I can't imagine. I'm sure it has been crazy hard. And I'm really sorry. You seem like you are doing well, though."

"Yeah. I guess. Anyway..." I say, deciding to get the topic off of me, "English, huh? What do you plan to do, teach?"

"Well, honestly, I'm not really sure. I just picked English because it was easy for me in high school. I absolutely hate science and I'm not great at math, so I'm trying to avoid anything that requires more than the minimum classes of those."

Chuckling, I agree. "Same, here. I got through them fine, but science and math are definitely not fun in my opinion."

"I'm hoping I'll eventually figure out what really interests me. I mean, I can teach, but it's not like that's been my life-long dream or anything. I figure I'll just keep working on getting all of the required classes out of the way and maybe by then, I'll know what direction to take," she says.

"I get that. I wasn't even planning to go to college. All I really wanted to do was get out of here and just experience the world a little," I tell Emily, trying not to wince at my new reality. Taking a deep breath, I continue, "But, since I'm kind of stuck here for now, I decided to take some art classes. It's been pretty fun."

I hear her smile, responding, "I've actually heard about your art,

Cal. I have a few friends who are in class with you, and they told me you made some really awesome sculptures. That's so cool."

I'm shocked that people are talking about my art. It's weird.

"Well, I don't know about all that, but I enjoy it."

All of a sudden, I feel someone smack me on my shoulder and sit right next to me. "What's up, dude? Looks like you're holding out on me." It's Ray. He sounds happy to see me, and a little too happy to annoy the shit out of me too.

I stick my hand out to him to shake his, but my sarcastic response makes him laugh. "What the fuck, Ray? I'm gonna kick your ass next time you do that." I continue, enjoying a somewhat normal moment with friends. "Ray, this is Emily. Emily, Ray." Hearing them exchange, "nice to meet you's," we go on to sit and chat for another hour.

It sounds like Ray and Emily are actually quite at ease with each other even though they just met. It's cool, though. I'm not laying claim.

BEFORE

"How long do you have?" I ask Sera, hoping she doesn't have to be home for a while.

"Well, I told dad I was going to be studying, so he just said to be home before 10:00," she says, a small smile sneaking through as she playfully bites the corner of her bottom lip. She's nervous but flirty, her thoughts exposed by the flush of her cheeks.

"You. Are. Killing me with that look, babe." My hand touches the side of her cheek, absorbing the heat between us. "Let's get out of here," I say, handing her the helmet. I climb on the bike and start it right before she jumps on behind me, immediately wrapping her arms around my chest.

And we are flying.

We drive for about thirty minutes before stopping at an old, abandoned lake house. I've been here before. Found it when I was out driving around last year. I can tell nobody has been here in a long time. It wouldn't be easy for a car to drive down the run-down road, the overgrown weeds camouflaging the winding, mile-long trail that leads to a small house with a rusted metal roof.

Still, I park in back before turning off the bike.

"What is this place?" Sera asks.

"I don't know. Just some place I found a while back. It's cool, though. Nobody lives here anymore. Looks like it's been years since anyone has been around. Is it ok? You don't have to be scared, but if you want to leave, we can."

"No, it's ok. Let's look around."

Grabbing her hand, we walk around to the side where there is an old wooden door aged with green paint flakes that curl up, barely hanging on, as if they are trying hard to preserve a beauty that once was. I push the door open. It's really not a bad place. Whoever left it didn't bother to take their furniture. Maybe they left in a hurry or at least planned to come back eventually, or maybe they won the lottery and traded all of their belongings for new. I don't know, but other than the cover of dust, the place is relatively clean and inviting, despite the obvious mysterious air about it.

Our hands still tightly woven, I pull Sera to the living room where a red, green, and gold plaid couch sits on a hard wood floor. An old wood stove decorates one corner, and an oval, antique rug sits in the center of the room beneath a table made out of petrified wood pieces with a glass top. The bookshelf in the corner holds a small library of what looks like a collection of some sort, hardbacks bound in blue and green with gold stripes.

We sit down on the couch, but Sera is on the edge, seemingly afraid to move back and get comfortable.

"Are you sure you are ok, Sera? We can leave if this place is scaring you. I know it's kind of weird, but I promise you are safe with me. At least here, we can just chill and not worry about someone seeing us." I hold my arm out, hoping she will relax against me.

Scooting closer to me, she rests her head on my chest and curls into me, her feet tucked beneath her. "I do feel safe with you, Cal. I really do. But this place *is* kind of freaky. I mean, it's just weird that it's out here and there is no one around. Are you sure we are allowed to be in here?" she asks, looking up at me.

"I don't think it really matters that we are in here, Sera. There's nobody to ask. Nothing has changed in here since I was here a year ago. There are no signs of anyone even messing around. And I've looked; there is no evidence that anyone actually lives here anymore, no refrigerator, beds, clothes or anything like that. It's like they just left the other stuff." I kiss the top of her head. "Let's just talk. I haven't seen you in too long; I'm having withdrawal, you know."

Her giggle makes me smile. "Ok. What do you want to talk about then?"

"Hmmm, how about...how much you've missed me?" Before she can answer, I'm tickling her and she is screaming and laughing.

"Stop. Oh my gosh. Stop. I'm so going to get you back," she says, recovering.

"Oh *really*? Then maybe I need to do it again." I jump up, playfully.

But she laughs and stops me, standing up to kiss my lips gently, before pulling back bashfully.

"Come here." Softly, I pull her back toward me. "A little closer..." Our faces are about an inch apart.

"Is this close enough?" she asks, looking up at me from under her eyelashes.

I whisper, "no," and then my lips take hers, removing every single fragment of doubt or fear. My heart feels torn between a sense of urgency and being content. It's like I can't get enough of her, but I don't want to push her too far either.

"More," she whispers when I pull back.

"More what, Sera?"

"Just...more," she says, kissing me again more fervently.

Our tangled bodies fall together onto the couch, mine carefully on top of hers as my arms prevent my weight from crushing her. "I don't want to hurt you, Sera."

"You won't, Cal. Please. Just be with me."

"Ok, baby, ok," I say, our souls touching, colliding.

And we realize a fire that doesn't singe.

It radiates.

Sparks mingle, igniting more as they dance.

We dance.

Flames lick, tasting, sensing each other

Our bodies are moving, loving, desperate. Frenzied.

More. More. More.

Ecstasy.

Euphoria.

A consummation of our emotions, of our youth, of our love.

Melding us now, and forever.

We lie side-by-side, no space between us. She is so beautiful.

After a few minutes, I face her, and wipe away a tear as it falls from her eye. "Are you ok?"

"I'm just happy, Cal. I promise," she says as her tears continue to flow more freely. "I love you, Cal. I love you so much. Just hold me."

"Baby, I love you, too. More than you will ever know," I say, kissing her forehead. "I've never felt this way before. It's like, I truly don't feel like I can live without you. Can't get you close enough to me. I will hold you, babe. Right now, and forever my sweet, Serafina."

And even as the sun sets and we are on our way back to her house, our light flickers, immune to the world around us.

PART II

Sera

CHAPTER 17

BEFORE

Feeling hope
Shattered
Seeing happiness
Mirage
I taste fear
Dreams
The sound of alarms
Emotions
A scent of dreams
Destruction

I CAN'T REMEMBER. My mind searches, reaches, tries to process the maze of recent memories. Lost, I can't find my way. Cal. We were going to study. Dad was at work, so I told my stepmom I would be back later.

But then.

What happened?

A sense of fear overcomes me, causing my body to tremble. But when I open my eyes, my anxiety heightens.

Pink wallpaper serves as a veneer. Pretending, deceiving, yet unable to conceal the machines, tubes, supplies, the numb mood that overwhelms me.

Turning my head to the side, I see my father sleeping on a makeshift bed. It's some kind of vinyl chair that extends. He doesn't look comfortable, but he is sleeping soundly.

So I lie here, in the quiet room that contradicts the screaming in my mind. Pulling the blankets up to my chin, I long for comfort, for safety. But the monsters continue to linger; they settle deep within me whispering, convincing me, preventing calm.

Until I can't take it anymore.

"Daddy?" I whisper it at first.

"Daddy. Dad." My voice becomes urgent.

"Sera?" He quickly stands and rushes to my side.

Grabbing my hand, he supports me, asking, "Hey, honey. How are you feeling?"

"What happened? Where am I?" I question him, hoping for clarity.

"Just relax. We've gone over this. Remember? You're ok now. You had an accident, but you are going to be just fine. We have to stay here a little longer, though. Ok? That way, the nurses and doctors can help you."

Suddenly aware of pain in my abdomen, I touch it, feeling for the source.

"It's ok. Leave that alone, Sera. The doctors had to remove your spleen and repair a few things, but your prognosis is great."

"What?" Panic consumes me again. "But it still hurts. How long have I been here?"

"Only a week, darling. You also suffered fractures in both legs, so you will be discharged to rehab when the doctors clear you, so just hang in there. I'm not leaving you."

I'll never leave you. Cal.

"Wait. Where is Cal? Is he ok? I don't remember anything. Dad, I think I was with him. We were going to study."

"He's fine. You don't need to worry about him."

"Can I see him?" I remember Dad didn't want me to be with Cal, but this is important. I have to see him. I have to. "Dad! I need to see him. Please take me to him."

"I'm sorry, Sera, but you can't do that right now. You were airlifted to a bigger hospital. Ok? There are specialists, experts here. I only want the best for you."

"Ok. Well, when can we leave? I need to be with Cal."

My father's clipped response reveals his feelings; "No, Sera. Right now, we are going to focus on getting you better."

Tears threaten to spill, but I try to contain them. I'm trapped, but I will find my way. To him.

"Fine, Dad, but just know that as soon as I'm better, I will go see him. Could you at least somehow let him know I'm ok and that I'm thinking about him? I don't want him to worry."

"Ok. I'll see what I can do." Unfortunately, I don't know if I can believe him. And it hurts me. My dad has always taken care of me. Always been there. But right now, I'm afraid he doesn't know what is best for me. He doesn't want to let me go. I love him, but Cal *is* my love. My future. He promised me he would never let me go, and I plan to hold him to that promise.

My anxiety abated, determination makes room in my mind giving me courage and fueling my desire to find my way back to Cal, to my home.

But my thoughts and memories remain foggy, clouding my path for a long time.

NOW

I'm running.

Away from my past. From my current. Out of reach of my father. To Cal.

But I'm scared. What if he hates me now? I haven't talked to him in eight months. He's probably moved on by now, but I have to know. If he still loves me like I love him.

He was my ticket to freedom.

My father's control stifled me, smothered me, and while I know he loves me, he's been slowly extinguishing my flame, depleting my oxygen so that I couldn't breathe.

Despite my perseverance throughout the long recovery, rehab has been challenging. Not only were my legs severely broken in more than one place, but my right knee required multiple surgeries to repair a ruptured ligament, torn meniscus, and several other issues that I can't remember in detail. I just remember the Dr. telling me that my knee looked like it had exploded and that it was the worst he had seen in his many years of practice. Also, being confined to a hospital bed caused my muscles to atrophy. I practically had to learn to walk all over again, and it's still not pretty. I finally graduated from using a walker to using a cane, but I'm still slow-moving and have a pretty pronounced limp.

I was supposed to continue with outpatient physical therapy for another six months at least, but I plan to try to do it on my own. I know what exercises to do.

My dad will be looking for me, but I'm not his little girl anymore. He needs to let me go.

In the three car garage attached to Dad's new house, my Bronco waits patiently for me. I haven't driven in so long. Although many of our belongings still remain boxed up, I know my Dad put my keys in his office desk drawer.

After the accident, my father sold our house and moved to Dallas where I have been receiving treatment. He says it's just easier and that he wanted to move here when I started college anyway. *Ugh.* The lengths he has gone to keep me away from Cal are getting ridiculous, but until now, I've played along, secretly planning my escape.

And today is the day.

I smile when I find my keys. The little plastic, yellow tag on my keyring reminds me of when I left my Bronco at the shop where Cal worked. I remember watching him write "blue Bronco" on it, their way to identify different sets of keys.

I had seen Cal in school multiple times. I never felt brave enough to talk to him, but I knew he worked at an auto shop. *I might have stalked him just a little. I mean, holy shit, he was hot.* I'll never forget his face when I got out of my car. He just stared at me. In jeans and a white t-shirt with grease on his face and clothes, he walked slowly to my Bronco, and I felt like I might die, like I was on fire. I couldn't look away, and even though I felt nervous, I smiled, and I swear I saw him flinch. I just hoped it was for a good reason.

I kept that tag on my keyring. Dad asked me about it once, but I just told him I forgot to ever take it off. Thankfully, he didn't have a clue. Because, honestly, from that moment, I planned to keep everything related to Cal from then on.

Last night I packed my suitcase. I have a ton of clothes and shoes, but obviously I can't take everything with me, so I picked about a week's worth of outfits. Along with my cosmetics, a picture of my family, and a stuffed bear that I've had since I was little, my clothes barely fit inside the rolling suitcase I just got last year for Christmas. I've been taking cash out of my account and saving it for this moment. I don't want to have to use my cards because they will just serve as a map for my dad to find me. I have around a thousand dollars. Even though it seems like a lot, I'm scared it will go fast, so I hope to get a job once I get settled.

My dad left for a meeting an hour ago. He works from home most of the time but occasionally has to go to the office, so this is my big chance to do this.

I'm really nervous, afraid that I will fail, but my desire to be on my own and get to Cal drives me to jump in my car, back out of the garage, and go.

A fresh start.

CHAPTER 18

BEFORE

"Stop. Stop! Please; it hurts so badly." Tears streak my face, a trail of pain.

"Sera, we have to do this. Just hang in there. We will get through it together," I hear my father say by my side.

I feel like I'm going to pass out while the nurses try to get me sit up in my bed. My legs hurt; my stomach hurts. Oh my God. I need it to stop. And I can't push my morphine button yet.

"It's important that you sit up, Sera," a nurse tells me.

"Why does it hurt so much? What is wrong with me?" I ask them, feeling confused.

"Remember, you were in an accident Sera. It's all going to be ok. Try to relax. We are going to take good care of you," she says.

I vaguely remember having a conversation with my dad about an accident. Closing my eyes, I try to calm down while I listen to my dad talk to the nurses quietly. I hear him asking them why I can't remember and they tell him it's normal, that it could be the medicine.

I try to raise my hand to ask how long I will be here, but I feel so tired; I can't get the words out.

"She's not even making sense, though," I hear him say.

And then I guess I'm dreaming because I'm on the motorcycle with Cal, driving on a long road that winds around. It's so fun. I love holding on to him. I feel safe with him, and the cool wind blows my hair back below the helmet, while we pass trees on either side of us. It's beautiful right now. All of the trees are blooming and there are wildflowers along the side of the road. Bluebonnets stand out among yellow, orange, and red flowers painting fields during tree breaks. We pass a ranch where horses play behind white fences near a red barn.

I feel like I'm in heaven.

But I shouldn't hurt in heaven. And the beeps... Did I set an alarm? I need to find it to turn it off, but I can't move my arms. My body is heavy.

Then I feel sad. Overwhelmingly sad. Cal is sad. He's telling me goodbye. I don't understand.

"No. No, you said you would never leave me. Don't go."

I hear my father telling me he's right beside me, but I'm not talking to him. Why is he here?

"Cal. Cal, stop." He's walking away. I see the bike on the ground and I'm standing in a pool of blood, and he's leaving me. "Where are you going? Don't leave me here. Please!"

I can hear myself screaming, begging.

Cal looks devastated when he turns around to face me from afar. He extends his hand to me, and all he says is, "I'm sorry."

"Sera, your dinner tray is here. Wake up, pretty girl."

My eyes slowly open, and the pink walls that still surround me make me nauseous.

"I don't want it."

My dad continues, "Come on. You've got to eat to get better. Just a few bites. Look. You have chicken noodle soup. You love that."

He holds the spoon to my mouth, feeding me like I'm a baby. I feel a little more awake, so I insist I can do it, but after about three bites, I'm physically drained. My dad takes the spoon again, helping me with the rest.

"Thank you, Daddy."

"You're welcome, sweetheart. Do you want to watch some TV? Or can I get you anything?"

"Can you get Cal?" I can't even look at him because I fear his answer.

"No, and we are not going to discuss it again. Ok?" The finality in his voice grates on me.

Frustrated, irritated, motivated.

Bring on the pain. Whatever it takes.

I DO NOT WANT to be confused anymore, so I refuse the morphine.

"On a level of one to ten, what is your pain level, Sera?" They ask me this several times a day. "We don't want you to be in pain."

I'm already in pain.

"Four," I tell her. "Can I just have some Tylenol or something?"

"Sure, but if you need more than that, it's ok. This is not the time to try and be tough. I can see you wince when we move you."

"I'll be fine. I don't like the way morphine makes me feel," I tell her, hoping that will be enough to convince her.

"Ok, but if you change your mind, you know you can just push the call button and one of us will be down here to help you." She leaves the room, pumping the hand sanitizer container next to the door before she exits. I realize their need to prevent germs, and I'm appreciative, but every time I see them do that, it annoys me a little. Makes me feel like I'm gross or something, like they want to clean their hands of me.

I've been in the hospital for a little over two weeks, and I don't think Dad has left me alone for one second. I have no idea how or when he is going home to change and freshen up.

"Dad, you don't have to stay here you know," I tell him. He's sitting by the window in his usual spot, reading a newspaper. It's kind of weird because, although that sounds normal, we don't get a paper at home anymore. Apparently, someone delivers a newspaper to each room in the hospital daily.

It kind of reminds me of when I was little, when Mom would sit on her chair doing crossword puzzles and Dad would read the newspaper by the large window, the drapes open to allow natural light into our sitting room. I remember running into the room with my dress shoes on, begging them to watch me dance. The clicking of my shoes echoed loudly on the tile floor, amplifying a sure-to-be grand performance. Mom's encouraging smile, my reward, inspired many turns and spins until my father would finally send me to play or practice some more. I was five years old. I remember because that was when my Mom signed me up for dance classes.

The rattle of paper and a grunt of acknowledgement is all I hear as Dad turns the page and straightens the newspaper that blocks all but the top of his head.

"Dad. Seriously. I'm fine here. Hey, and when you go home, can you bring me my cell phone and my kindle?" I'm so bored. I want to call Chasity. And Cal, but I don't know how to reach him. I don't know a phone number or address, and the shop where he worked used cell phones only. I'm hoping Chasity can help with that though.

"I'm not going home right now, Sera, and I've already told you, your phone was broken in the accident. I will try to remember to get your kindle next time I go home, though."

Oh my God. I guess it makes sense that my phone would have broken, but I don't know what to do. It had all of my contacts in it and I don't remember numbers for anyone. *When did he tell me about my phone anyway?*

"Sera, we need to talk about something anyway," he says, finally putting the paper down and making eye contact with me. He sounds too serious, which makes me nervous.

"What is it?" I ask him while staring down and wringing my hands.

Recognizing my normal response when anxious, Dad walks to my bedside. "It's nothing to worry about, but Dr. Adler said it's time for another knee surgery. You've had a couple of surgeries already, and you may need several more before this is all over. You are scheduled to go in tomorrow early morning."

"Why does the Dr. only tell you these things? I am capable of making decisions for myself. What if I don't want another surgery?" I ask him defiantly. I'm so tired of this. All of it. The pain. Being trapped here. It stinks so badly.

"Sera," he says in that voice, the one that says, "Chill out and listen to reason." I hate that condescending voice right now.

"What? You don't understand, Dad. I hate this."

"I know you hate this, but you have to get through it. This surgery is needed to further repair your knee, and you are just going to have to trust Dr. Adler — and me. It's not fun for me either, you know. I hate seeing my little girl in pain. But I'm here with you, and we just have to do what the doctors tell us. I told Dr. Adler to let me be the one to tell you. You have had a few memory issues, Sera, and you haven't been yourself, but everyone assures me that will all resolve over a little more time. Your brain just experienced some trauma, and I'm doing the best I can to help you get better. Ok? Just calm down and everything will be fine."

Damn these erratic tears that fall without permission.

"Fine." I don't want to talk anymore.

Feelings of defeat deflect any ounce of positivity I had a moment ago. How will I ever break free from this hell hole?

NOW

My first stop: to buy a burner phone. I left the cell phone that Dad bought me on the table beside my bed in my room. He clearly has restrictive settings on my phone. Tracking me by my phone would be too easy.

Navigating the wild Dallas streets and traffic is not exactly comforting. I hope I can avoid big highways for the most part even if it takes me longer to get somewhere.

I'm so out of my element here.

My father's new neighborhood is beautiful, full of older houses and huge trees. I've obviously paid attention when Dad has taken me out to eat or to physical therapy, but I really haven't been out much. Admittedly, I've remained somewhat reclusive considering my difficulty getting around. I used to enjoy shopping, but obviously that would be challenging and hardly fun without friends.

Before she passed away, my mother took me shopping and on various outings all the time. Dad was a workaholic, so our girly time was very special to me.

When I was older, Chasity and I used to go shopping on weekends all the time. Sometimes her mom would take us out to eat or to a movie, too. It meant a lot to me that Chasity included me after mom died. Chasity was more like a sister to me, even though she could be annoying at times. I guess that's part of being a sister though. I can't wait to see her again. I'm sure she thinks I fell off the face of the earth after eight long months with no communication.

The bullseye Target sign welcomes me like a beacon, standing out among other familiar logos and symbols that represent the life I had before. Texas Roadhouse. Gap. PacSun. Chic-fil-A. Cinnabon. Starbucks.

I'm not a huge coffee drinker, but a cinnamon roll and a smoothie would seriously make this journey better right now. After stopping to get a phone and a few other essentials, I plan to drive through the Cinnabon near the entrance to Target.

Even though I want to be careful with my money, I decide to invest in the more expensive burner phone of the three choices. I'm sure some of the apps on the smart phone will come in handy, google maps being especially important.

I also grab a few snacks: barbeque chips, Junior Mints, Sour Punch straws, and some powdered sugar doughnuts, and of course a big bottle of water and a 20 oz. Diet Dr. Pepper. Obviously, I want a little of everything and my dad hasn't been buying me sweet stuff. I love candy, so I feel a little giddy loading my bags into my Bronco.

A good road trip requires good snacks.

With my Google map open, I enter my destination, and 258 miles separate me from my real home. From my old life and my new life. Everything in between has been a nightmare.

AFTER OVER AN HOUR OF DRIVING, I'm finally leaving the bigger city with five-lane highways and crazy traffic. I think maybe I can breathe now. At one point, four people on motorcycles flew past me probably going at least a hundred miles an hour. It made me so sick to my stomach that I had to pull over at the next gas station and get out of the car for a minute. Seeing motorcycles has already bothered me, but when Dad was driving somewhere, if I saw one, I just looked away and tried to think of something else. I couldn't do that while driving, and the idea of them going so fast after what Cal and I went through is horrifying. I don't think I will ever be able to ride again, which saddens me because it was so beautiful, but in the end, I just don't know if I would be able to feel safe enough to not freak out.

They weren't the only ones who passed me going super-fast, or who weaved around me like I had no idea how to drive. I mean, God, I was still going the speed limit. Seventy miles per hour isn't exactly slow. It all just proved to me that such a large city isn't for me.

I never thought I would look forward to seeing fields of cotton, mesquite trees, and prominent, giant wind turbines, and with each little town through which I travel, more and more comforting road-sides greet me.

I even smile at a dead rattlesnake on the road. The smile turns into laughter, which turns into tears. My emotions are all over the place. I feel scared, happy, relieved, nervous, anxious, elated, free.

Since my old Bronco doesn't have a great radio, I had been driving in silence. It's either that or listen to static-y country music that I really think consists of all of the songs on albums that never made it. I've wondered before how they come up with their playlists. It's weird. Like, are there only eighty-year-old cowboys who listen to the radio around here?

My new phone doesn't have my music on it, so I decide to sing. Thankfully, nobody is with me so I can sing out and not worry about it, but I have to admit, even I cringe when I miss a note. I'm an ok singer, but when I sing loud, it's not great.

I listened to a lot of music in the hospital, but for some reason, dumb kid songs keep coming to my mind. Maybe it's because I know all of the words to those songs, but I giggle when I sing, "If You're Happy and You Know It," while honking instead of clapping. I'm pretty sure I'm a dork, but it's ok because I'm a happy dork. At least at the moment.

CHAPTER 19

BEFORE

Waking up from anesthesia sucks. The bright lights above me offend my blinking eyes, a deluge of confusion suspending recovery while I lie in a bed with too warm blankets too tightly tucked around me.

In and out, my mind wanders from a dream-like state to reality. One second I think I'm stuck in quick sand, and when the nurse tells me to be still and relax, I think, oh yeah, I'm not supposed to move in quick sand or it will pull me further under. But lying still is horribly annoying. I hate feeling trapped. I can't even talk. I hear my words not come out like I intend.

Moans take place of my pleading to be able to move my hands and legs. Again, the nurse's voice, "Just relax. You're doing so well. The doctor said everything went well. Are you in any pain?"

I don't think I am. Am I? Shaking my head, I continue to try to convince her to remove the heavy, hot, stupid, freaking blankets.

Finally, I am alert enough to speak, but by then, nausea has overcome me.

"Please take the blankets off. I'm hot. I think I'm gonna puke. Hurry. Please."

Not quickly enough, she finally uncovers my body and hands me an emesis basin. I barely make it.

Vomiting after surgery is not my favorite thing to do. All of my muscles tighten up, and then the pain from my surgery hits hard, making me even more nauseous.

With a wet, cold rag, the nurse wipes my forehead and places it against the back of my neck. She also injects something into the iv port in my forearm explaining that it will help me to relax and settle my stomach.

Within minutes, I feel more calm. It is such a relief. Ever since my mom passed away, I have struggled with anxiety. It is the worst feeling in the world to have a panic attack. The problem is, physical pain somehow makes me feel anxious, and then anxiety makes me feel physical pain. It's a vicious cycle of horror. I've seen counselors and been on medicine for it for years now, but sometimes the pain, whatever triggers it, causes my anxiety to take over, and I hate it.

Cal always made me feel calm. I don't know what it was about him, but it just felt so right to be with him. But the idea of losing him always lingered in the back of my mind, and now it feels like it's actually happening.

I lost my mom. I don't want to lose Cal.

And even though I love my dad, I'm not going to be his little girl forever. He doesn't understand my anxiety though. He thinks I should get over it, that I know better so I should be able to control it. I've tried to explain it to him, to tell him that even when I understand and *know better*, sometimes a panic attack can still happen. My last counselor said I probably have triggers and that I need to journal so that I can figure out what they are, so I started journaling at age 12.

Writing in my journal has always been a comfort to me. I'm able to pour my soul into words, put my fears on paper, which somehow allows me to let them go, at least a little. Every night before bed, I wrote.

Until my dad found my journals, and it was hell.

~

I WAS NEVER able to spend as much time with Cal as I wanted to, so one night, I told Dad I would be spending the night with Chasity. We were planning to go to a party anyway, so I asked Cal to go with us. Dad probably wouldn't have approved of my going to a party with or without Cal, but I definitely didn't plan to mention any of it to Dad. Even though I knew he was over protective, he trusted me. I think he believed I was his little puppet, that he had trained me well.

Then he read the last journal entry I ever wrote:

Dear Amy, (I always wrote in letter style and Amy was my mom's middle name)

Tonight was crazy. I spent the night with Chasity and we went to a party in Mesa Hills. It's such a pretentious neighborhood, but our friends said they were going, so we decided to go, too, even though I don't really know the guy whose house it was. Anyway, Cal went with us, and we were hanging out with everyone. Cal had his arms around me. It was so deliciously awesome just being close to him. I felt him kiss me on the top of my head and since he was behind me, his breath in my ear when he talked was so hot, I pretty much thought I was going to die. Oh my God. He's so sexy, and sweet, and, yeah...

So, we were talking and everything was fine, until stupid dick-head Chance came up and started in on Cal. God, he's such a jerk. That's why I only dated him for a couple of weeks. He's Dad's rich friend's son, so apparently, he thinks he can do whatever he wants. He was drunk and extremely rude, and then all of a sudden, he and Cal were fighting. Well, he was too drunk to be able to land a punch, but Cal was beating the hell out of him. Honestly, it was kind of hot, but I was a little scared because Cal looked pissed, and he looked like he could really hurt Chance. I started screaming for them to stop. I didn't want Cal to get in trouble, and even though I seriously don't like Chance, I didn't exactly want him to die. Then, Cal took off walking super-fast. I looked around, trying to figure out what to do. Chance was moving so he was probably fine, and I didn't want Cal to leave, so I took off after him.

He was apparently starting to walk home. I grabbed him and told him to stay. I felt so embarrassed that my friends were horrible, and I felt guilty for subjecting Cal to their ugliness. It sucked. But when I told him I was sorry, he freaked out and started apologizing to me. He wasn't even worried about them. He said he was only worried about what I thought about him.

I'm so glad he didn't leave. I held his hand all the way home. I wanted to talk to him more but Chasity was with us. She was even being rude, but I don't think she meant anything by it. I've learned to deal with her when she is too open and blunt, but hopefully Cal didn't feel offended.

I really haven't known Cal very long, and Dad cautioned me after meeting Cal that night that he came over. It pisses me off that people, and especially my dad, act like Cal isn't good enough for me. I feel like we have this crazy strong connection, and it's like our souls fit together. He's really so beautiful. He's kind, smart, funny, and obviously hot as hell.

Honestly, I'm pretty sure I love him. God, I do love him. So much. I don't think I'm being crazy either. If Mom were here, I bet she would love Cal, too.

I can't wait to see him tomorrow.

Sera ~ Cal forever

Love,

Sera

I DID SEE Cal that next day. We kissed and it was beautiful and sexy and so perfect. But when I got home that night, Dad was waiting for me. He was sitting in the living room holding my journal. When I saw him, I was furious. I could not believe he would do that. That he would read my private thoughts. I'll never forget what he said either. I asked him, "How could you do that?" He actually said, "I had to, Sera, and I'm glad I did. You can't be around Cal anymore. He's not good for you, he's not like you, and he's just going to be trouble. I'm sorry, but I'm putting my foot down. If I have to, I will ground you, but I hope you will respect my wishes and trust my judgement. This is over. I've talked to Chance's dad and he's not going to press charges, but if I find out you are hanging out with that boy again, he might just end up in jail."

I was shocked. How could he stoop that low? It was like he didn't even care how I felt. But I didn't want anything bad to happen to Cal, and I knew how manipulative my dad's rich friends could be. I left Cal a note the next day, and it was the hardest thing I ever had to do.

I would never trust my dad again. Ever. I was more determined than ever to graduate and get away.

"How are you feeling?" My dad's voice is soothing, but I feel conflicted after the overwhelming memory of that night. It's like all of those emotions came rushing back: anger, disappointment, frustration, hurt.

"I'm fine." I answer. I don't feel like elaborating.

"Is your knee hurting?"

"It's fine."

"Sera, what's going on? You seem angry."

My sarcastic response in my mind probably won't help anything, so I just deny it.

"I said I'm fine. Ok?"

Before he can speak, a nurse and Dr. Adler come into the room. Dad stands to greet them, but I still feel gripy, so I just sit in my uncomfortable hospital bed in silence.

"Hello, Sera," Dr. Adler says. "How are you feeling?"

My God. How many times have I been asked that just today alone? And do they want the honest answer? Because I doubt it.

"I'm fine." It's apparently my new phrase for the day.

Dr. Adler begins unwrapping my knee. "I just need to check the site. Ok? Any pain right now?"

"Yes." He looks up at me from my knee, his eyebrows raised a bit indicating his recognition of my agitation.

"Ok. On a scale of 1 to 10, what is your level of pain right now?"

"Maybe a 6?" I don't know. I don't feel like freaking talking. I just want to sit here and be irritated. Thinking that elicits a small grin. I know sarcasm isn't polite, but oh well.

The doctor tells the nurse to give me some medicine. Now that he's messed with it, I'm thinking it's more like an 8, so I'm thankful, even though I don't say anything.

Wrapping it back up, Dr. Adler speaks again. "Alright. I want you to rest tonight, but tomorrow we are going to do some exercises and move it. You won't be able to walk or anything for several more weeks, and even then we will have to play things by ear, but I believe if we move slowly, your prognosis is good. Ok? So just hang in there and I'll be back in tomorrow afternoon to check on you." He leaves the room, and I'm glad he doesn't insist on a response from me. I really don't feel like talking right now. I just want the pain to go away.

All of it.

NOW

My leg is achy after driving for so long. The knee brace keeps my leg too stiff, so I'm driving without it, and God, it's starting to really hurt. Opening my water bottle, I pop three ibuprofen in my mouth and swallow. I've been taking them pretty regularly. It's probably not healthy, but at least it doesn't make me feel weird like the Tylenol with codeine. The temporary relief of pain medications they gave me in the hospital caused bad dreams. Confused and conflicted illusions danced in my paralyzed state. Tingly needles of fiction provoked me while imprisoning me for its four to six hours of half-life.

I'm only about thirty minutes from town now. I recognize where I am so the google map is finally off. While it's helpful, the lady's voice was starting to get annoying. Plus, I was talking back to her, sometimes arguing with her, which makes me question my sanity a little too much.

I know I've changed after this whole ordeal. I just hope I can be normal again. Right now, it still seems too far away.

Thirty minutes.

Will I see Cal? How will I even find him? Like, will he just be around town and I'll see him and I'll be like, "hey."? I don't have any idea if he will even want to see me. I mean, I think he will. It's not my fault I couldn't talk to him.

God, and I really don't love the idea of seeing old friends, except for Chasity of course. I have this discernable limp which totally sucks.

My thoughts are running wild.

ALTHOUGH I'VE HAD eight long months to plan my escape, I failed to decide exactly where I want to stay. I know my father will look here first, and because this is a relatively small town, it probably won't take him too long to find me. However, I want to prolong the inevitable as long as I can, so after driving through town, I remember the lake house where I went with Cal. I'm way too scared to stay there by myself, but I remember we passed some rental cabins on the way.

The Red Hawk Cabins, actually brown, appear run-down and desolate. A faded red neon sign glows "vacant" in the window of the office, persuading me to be brave and enter. Despite my nerves, I suck it up and open the door to a dim paneled office where a man with a huge beard sits behind a yellow counter. The bell on the door, a superfluous alert of my presence at this moment, elicits an uninterested reaction from the man. Without looking up from his book, he asks, "What can I do for ya?"

"Um, I was wanting to check on renting a cabin?" Lacking confidence, I sound unsure.

"Well, they're all empty right now as you can see. How long ya need it for?"

"I'm not sure yet. I just need a place to stay temporarily. How much would it be to rent for a month?"

"Don't normally rent 'em out by the month. Seein' how it's the low season though, we might be able to work something out. You hidin' from something?" He still hasn't looked at me. I don't know how he would even know.

"No sir." I lie. His eyes slowly wander up to meet mine and he scoffs. "Hmph. Ain't no young girls come 'round here to stay. You got to be hidin' from something. You can park your truck in the back. Cabin C will probably be as good as any," he says, pointing towards the back of the group of about ten cabins. I turn my head towards that direction and nod.

"Yes. Thank you. How much?" I have a little over $700 left after gas and Target. Without meaning to, my wringing hands convey my concern.

"How's about $300 for the month? Can you manage that?"

"Yes, sir. That sounds great. Thank you," I say again, pulling out exactly $300 to hand over the counter.

"Welp, looks like you got you a place to stay now. Here's the key. You'll need to sign here." He slides a generic contract over and points to a pen, attached to the counter with a silver beaded string and duct tape. After signing the paper and taking the key, I head back to my car. He yells out before the door closes, "Don't want no trouble, though. Ya hear?"

Nodding again behind me, I jump in my Bronco and drive around to park behind Cabin C, my new place.

"Home sweet home," I mutter as I enter the not so welcoming abode. Again with the old décor, the chair and couch look like they jumped out of the seventies, similar to the lakehouse where Cal took me. The dingy white tiled floor is camouflaged with little brown and black specs, maybe to better hide dirt. A taxidermied fish takes up about two feet on the wall above the couch. It looks like it was caught years ago, covered in dust and a few cobwebs, the fins a faded yellow and orange with silver streaks.

"What?" I ask it. It stares back at me, dumbly. "You sure are ugly." I tell it before throwing a t-shirt over it. I don't like being watched, even by a thirty-year-old, dead fish.

The small wooden dresser in the corner holds the contents of my suitcase quite well. I'm so glad I threw my soft blanket and pillow into the car before leaving because the bedspread is scratchy and God knows when it was washed last.

A small tv sits on the dresser. I'm kind of surprised to get any channels when I turn it on, but the noise is extremely comforting. I'm not used to being completely alone.

It's already dark at seven since it's January. I check the bolt lock on the door one more time. Peeking out the window, the moon casts a glow on the trees around the lake. Tomorrow, I plan to explore. I want to find Cal, but I'm scared. I need to get re-acclimated to this life.

CHAPTER 20

BEFORE

Although I've been unable to put weight on my legs, the nurses and physical therapists force me to move from the bed to a chair daily, and today my dad wheeled me to the hospital cafeteria in a wheelchair. A nightgown and robe make for embarrassing out-to-eat attire, but there are other patients escaping their rooms just like me. One guy was in line only wearing socks and his hospital gown. Thank goodness he didn't turn his back to me. Surely he was wearing underwear, but it was super awkward and I'm totally good with never seeing his or any other patients' butts, naked or not, especially considering the patients here are all older than me. Gross. And I hope he changed his socks when he got back to his room. We're in a hospital. It disgusts me to think of all the germs he acquired.

I still can't wear pants. I have athletic shorts on underneath my gown, but it's really a pain to put them on over the casts. I just couldn't stand the thought of going out of the room without them, but it won't be fun to deal with taking them back off later either. Today my nurse is a guy, too. I don't want his help or my dad's, so hopefully I can manage by myself.

It feels good to get out of my pink prison. Pepto Bismol pink walls equal pure torture.

Dad has brought food to me some so I don't always have to eat the hospital food, but since we are here, at least I can choose what I want. My tray is full.

"You're never going to be able to eat all of that." Dad cautions me.

"I'm gonna try," I respond. I couldn't help it. A cheeseburger and fries, side salad, banana pudding, and a rice crispy treat to go with my large Diet Dr. Pepper, all perfect choices if you ask me.

Thankfully, Dad smiles when he says, "I'm just happy to see you eating and out of that room. You're getting a little color back."

"I probably blended in with the unsightly walls in there," I say, giggling.

"You should be thankful I brought you here. This hospital is much nicer than most, and you could have been sharing a room with some crazy person if you weren't here."

"What do you mean, you brought me here? I thought you said I had to be here because the doctors were experts or something."

"Oh, they are, honey. It was definitely necessary."

"Necessary for you or for me, dad?" I ask him, looking right into his eyes as we arrange our food on the round table in the middle of the large room.

"For both of us, of course. Don't start jumping to conclusions, Sera. You needed to be here, so like I said, just be thankful for the good care you are receiving."

I definitely wouldn't have wanted to be in a room with someone else. It would be so weird to hear another person in pain. The power of suggestion alone would have made me feel like I shared in every single sickness. I'm one of those freaks who gags when someone else is throwing up, and if Chasity says she has a headache, I have to seriously talk myself down because I usually start feeling a headache coming on as well. It's silly, but my therapist says it's part of my OCD and anxiety. Embracing it as one of my *quirky* traits is a more flattering way of thinking about it, though.

"Dad, do we have to go back to the room yet?" I ask after we finish eating. I'm saving my rice crispy treat for later since it's wrapped. Dad was right. It was too much food, but God, it was a nice treat.

"Well, there is a courtyard downstairs. How about we go outside for a while? I bet we can find some shade since it's hot. The nurse told me to check in if we are going to be longer than an hour, so I'll call up to the floor and let her know what we were doing."

OH MY GOSH. The sun feels amazing. Its warmth brings about the biggest smile I think I've had in a month. Yellow flowers line the sidewalk leading to a large tree, under which sits a metal and wood slatted park bench. The tree is beautiful, the trunk alone probably eight feet around. Dad parks my wheelchair underneath the large branches, each covered in large, dark green leaves. Looking up into its canopy, I giggle while watching a couple of squirrels chasing each other, leaping from branch to branch in delight. God, to be free to jump and run again will be the most amazing gift. It's not something a person ever thinks about: being unable to walk or get around. I definitely took it for granted.

After my mother passed away, I never went back to a dance class again. I remember getting to dress up and Mom decorated my face with eye shadow, blush, and mascara before every recital. She always told me I was beautiful without it but that it helped people in the crowd to see me better. Dancing was fun, but the best part was spending time with my Mom. Once she was gone, it meant nothing to me.

However, right now, I really wish I could dance. The sounds, the smells, the beauty surrounding me outside frees my sadness. The oppressive gate opens and exchanges my tears for joy.

Large roots interrupt the concrete beneath the tree, spiraling around in their own little dance. Leaves blowing, birds singing. It's heaven. And I'm taking it all in. Reminded of my mom, and of my Cal. Somehow, being outside substitutes in a small way, filling the cracks caused by pain. The void in my soul is separated with a bookmark, awaiting reunification with my other half. Cal, and the rest of my life.

Pain is temporary. It is a cliché seized and clinched in my heart.

SWEAT DRIPPING down my face prompts the return to my room.

It actually feels good to elevate my legs in the bed again.

"Thank you for taking me out, Dad," I tell him, smiling.

"You're welcome, sweetheart. It's great to see you smile again. Hey, and I have a surprise for you. I was going to wait, but since this has already turned into such a great day, I think this will make it even better."

He reaches into his briefcase and pulls out a box. When placed on my lap, I am happy to receive a new phone. "Yay! I've been having withdrawal." I laugh.

"It's a newer version of the last one you had. I hope you enjoy it. I'm going to go home and change. I need to get a few things for work, but I'll be back in an hour. I programmed my number in the phone just in case you need me, but I promise I won't be long."

"Dad, I've told you before. It's fine. You don't need to spend every second with me here. Besides, I bet Megan would like to spend a little time with you too, you know." Megan, my stepmom, has visited me a few times, but usually my father monopolizes all of my time.

"Don't worry about Megan. You remember her sister and her family live here. She has enjoyed spending time with them."

Once he's gone, I open the box and check out my new phone. It dawns on me that I don't have numbers for any of my friends though. Chasity doesn't have the same last name as her mom because her mom remarried after divorcing Chasity's father years ago. I don't think they have a home phone anyway. I know Cal doesn't.

Shit. I have to figure out a way to reach them, but I need to do it while Dad's gone. *Dang it.*

Looking on the internet for a whole hour, I've come up with nothing. Facebook is freaking blocked. *Blocked!* I'm unable to get snap chat, Instagram, anything. I'm so pissed. It was just a ruse. Dad doesn't trust me, and damn it, I still don't trust him either.

NOW

Stretching my arms wide, my eyes open to the morning sun shining through the window. A small moment of confusion quickly transitions into realization. I'm free.

My knee is usually sore in the mornings so it takes me a minute to get dressed and get my tennis shoes on, but as soon as I'm ready, I step outside to take a look around. The winter breeze fills my senses with the smells of trees, the lake, and of home. Brings back memories. Of love, safety. Of giving myself to Cal.

Warmth fills my cheeks at the thought of my first and only intimate night with Cal. He was gentle but impatient. Caring but bold. Taking and giving.

Immersed.

Physically shaking my head as to snap out of it, I smile and wander around a bit more, familiarizing myself with my surroundings.

My goal today is to get a job. The limited amount of cash in my wallet will not sustain me for long. In addition, I need interaction with people again. Eight solitary months have been lonely and I want to rebuild my life here again. This is my home. I just hope I can find Cal and that he still wants me.

Wearing jeans with a cute, white button-up top dotted with tiny purple flowers, I feel dressed appropriately for the places for which I intend to apply.

My first stop is a small diner. It was a place I was supposed to meet Cal one time. Not only does it feel like a small connection to him, I hope he might eat here sometimes since he is the one who suggested it. As soon as I walk in the door, the smell of comfort food hits me at the same time an older waitress tells me from across the room to take a seat anywhere.

Gathering all of my courage, I walk towards her. "Thank you, ma'am. Actually, I was wondering if y'all are hiring, and if so, I would like to fill out an application."

I'm sure she noticed my limp when I came in, her eyes drifting downward giving her away. I just hope I can handle being on my feet all day.

"Have you ever waitressed before?" She's cleaning a table while talking to me, multitasking.

"Umm, no ma'am, but I'm a fast learner."

"Come talk to Jim in the back. He's the one you really need to convince," she says, leading the way.

"Yes, ma'am." I say, following. She turns her head back towards me while still walking, "And call me

Marge, honey."

"Oh, sure. Thank you, Marge." Seemingly kind, she looks like she's had a hard life. The lines around her lips reveal years of smoking, and her dyed reddish hair is ratted and pulled up, piled high on her head.

It's not a long walk to the back office considering the small size of the place, but she manages to fit in a decent conversation on the way.

"What's your name, hon?"

"Oh, yeah. Sorry. I'm Sera."

"I see. Are you from here? You look familiar."

"Well, yes and no. I used to be, but I just recently moved back." I never came in here before even though I lived in this small town for my whole life. My Dad kept me on the upper class side of the tracks, the figurative boundary separating us from everyone else. It's embarrassing. But I'm changing that now, changing myself. Recognizing truth and love.

"Hmm, I bet I'll figure it out before too long. Well, here's Jim's office." Marge knocks on the door before opening it slightly.

"Jim? You got a minute?"

"Come on in," he says through the door.

Opening it wider, she introduces me, "Jim, this here's Sera. She needs a job. Put her under me. I'll train her up right." She winks at me before leaving me alone with Jim.

"Hello. Thank you for seeing me," I speak, my voice sounding shy.

"Have a seat, Sera," he says, gesturing towards an old vinyl, yellowing chair with rollers on the bottom of it. I sit and pull it forward to the other side of his desk.

"So, why should I hire you, Sera?"

He looks at me above his glasses that are sliding down his nose, away from the large computer monitor atop his desk. There are papers everywhere along with a bookshelf behind him with notebooks and other clutter. A framed 5 x 7 picture of his presumed family sits on his desk next to a name plate that reads "Jim Clark."

"Well, sir, I'm a fast learner, and I'm good with people," I tell him, which is true when I'm comfortable enough.

"Uh-huh, and do you have any experience with being a waitress or working in a restaurant?"

"No sir. This would be my first job, sir. If you could just give me a chance, though, I promise I will do a good job. I work hard, and I know I can learn how to do everything quickly."

"It just so happens, Sera, that one of my waitresses called in sick today. How about you try it out today and we'll see how it goes. Can you work today?"

"Yes. That would be perfect, actually! Thank you so much. You won't regret it."

"Well, I've been thinking I could use another person around here. Gets pretty busy, though, so I hope you're up for it."

135

"I won't let you down, sir. Thank you again."

He's shooing me out the door, yelling for Marge to get me an apron before I can finish thanking him.

FALLING ON MY BED, I check my phone for the time. It's 10:30 PM. I worked all day. I was supposed to leave at 6:00, but I could tell they needed me for the night crowd, too. Marge was leaving, and there was only one waitress named Mandy coming in. She seemed ok. I think she appreciated my help, but she did seem a little annoyed when I made a few mistakes, like forgetting to refill Mr. Jordan's tea.

He's apparently a regular, comes in every evening at 7:05. He looks about eighty years old and brings a picture of his wife who Mandy told me passed away three years prior. The picture on one side of the table, he sits on the other. He eats his meal quietly, but he was pleasant to me, even when I did forget to get him some more tea. Left me a $5 tip, and his meal was only $7.50. When I delivered his plate of pecan pie after his meal of chicken fried steak, he thanked me and told me I reminded him of his wife. Said he could tell that I had a sweet spirit and that I was a fighter. Smiling, I thanked him. I was flattered that he would compare me to someone he so obviously revered, but thinking about it tonight, I wonder what he saw in me that made him say I'm a fighter. It was good to hear, though. Confirmation.

My feet definitely hurt after running back and forth from the kitchen to various tables, but surprisingly, my legs and knees are doing ok. Rubbing my feet after removing my tennis shoes feels good, but I'm exhausted. I don't even count the tip money I laid on the bedside table before falling sound asleep.

CHAPTER 21

BEFORE

Finally. After four long weeks in this pink hell that was closing in more and more each day, the nurse is discharging me.

"Sign on this line here." She marks an X next to the small space. "It's just saying that you received all of your discharge information."

Scribbling my name, I ask, "So, how long will I have to be at this next place?"

"That's up to you, Sera. You need to be sure to do everything they tell you and work hard, even when you get tired. It's rehab, and it may seem like they are trying to kill you, but I promise they will get you back to normal faster than you can say 'Run'." She smiles and winks at me.

"Ok, I'll do my best."

But I'm thinking, *Run*. And I'm pretty sure it won't be fast enough.

OH MY GOD. Huge floral yellow and blue printed wallpaper replaces my pink walls. *What did I hate about the color pink again?*

"Seriously, Dad? Is there some rule that medical facilities must be hideously decorated?"

"It's not that bad, dear. Maybe it will make you work harder," he says while placing a floral arrangement on the window sill, the fifth weekly gift of encouragement I've received from him throughout this ordeal.

Similarly, at home, fresh flowers adorn the dining table, changed every single week. Mom loved flowers. It's a tradition continued after she passed, but one that has grown to strangle me, stealing all of the air from the room, from the whole house, from my life.

"Dad, can you please stop bringing flowers?" Gesturing towards the walls, I say, "I mean, don't you think it's kind of floral overload in here?"

"You're mother always loved flowers. Said it brightens a room."

"Yeah, well, she's not here, and this room is *bright* enough. Please?"

"You are going to have to work on that attitude, Sera. *Stop Negativity*," he reads the ridiculous stop sign hanging near my bed.

Turning my head to look at the laminated sign tacked on the papered wall, I roll my eyes and sigh. My Dad's being a butt, his smirk indicating the humor at least *he* finds in the room.

"Seriously? This is so freaking stupid."

"What's so stupid?"

And in walks a welcoming committee of one. A guy so hot that I can't help the blush that slowly creeps up my face from below my neck, warmth announcing my feelings. *Could I be more obvious?* It's not like Cal disappeared from my mind or anything, but oh man. This dude is so hot. Tall with a little brown stubble to match his unfixed, yet adorable hair, adds to the light blue, fitted scrubs he is working with each step. I think he's actually strutting.

Embarrassed and feeling a little guilty for even noticing, I look down and pull at an imaginary string on my old, gray sweat pants. I'm wearing my comfortable, wear-at-home-only pants with a non-matching tank top.

I can feel Dad looking at me, surely noticing my reaction.

"She thinks your sign is stupid, and this room, and apparently everything right now."

And...my face is even hotter. *Thanks Dad.*

Sitting on my bed with my legs extended, I try to sink further into myself, when I'm suddenly interrupted by Super Stud sitting next to me on the edge of my bed. I can't help but look up. He's facing me, his right knee touching my leg. I would move to scoot over, but the hard wall next to my bed doesn't want to let me in, although at this moment, I would be totally cool with hiding behind the butt ugly flowers.

"*This,*" he says, accenting the word, "is not stupid. I'm not stupid, and I doubt you are either, so let's start fresh."

Dude, you and your chipper self are just a little too close for comfort. Sheesh.

"Whatever. This room *is* stupid," I say, sarcastically grinning at him.

"All I see is beauty," he replies, looking right at me.

Is he serious?

"I didn't get your name." I try to change the subject.

"I didn't tell you my name, but it's Brett since you're asking."

Hot or not, he's starting to irritate me. He clearly thinks highly of himself.

"Yeah, well, I'm just gonna chill here in my *beautiful* room and get settled. Thanks for umm, checking up on me." Unfortunately, my attempt to dismiss him backfires.

"Oh really? Don't let me intrude or anything." Then the crazy guy starts laughing. *What the hell?*

Dad and I look at each other for a second and then watch him, waiting for him to chill the crap out.

"Yeah, so..." I try again.

Pulling out a small pad of paper from his pocket, he says, "Sera, right?"

I nod and continue to wait him out.

"Great. Let's get busy. You don't get *free* days here. Can you get up to walk or do you need assistance? I'm going to take you on a tour of this *non-stupid* place."

"Dude, I just got here."

"Uh-huh. Now let's get moving." He stands from my bed and reaches out for my hand.

Ignoring him, I tell him I don't need his help, even though I do kind of want to hold his hand regardless of his sarcastic, over-confident butt-head personality. He's *that* cute, and I've had nobody to talk to besides Dad for the most part.

"Fine," I tell him, but it *is* actually really hard for me to do this alone. I grab the walker that I left within reach and slowly swing my legs to the side of the bed, gently pushing my right knee with my hand.

Distracted by the warm hand on the back of my left shoulder, I look up at him, as if to remind him of my independence, but he leaves it there. And the battle is on.

Flashing my fake, sarcastic smile again, I am determined to get out of here sooner than later, or at least prove to Mr. Hotty McGee that I'm not an invalid in the meantime.

"I've got work to do so I'll stay here while you go do your thing," Dad tells me. Giving him a quick annoyed look, I immediately concentrate on holding on to my walker so that I don't fall. My knee feels weak, and it seriously hurts to walk or move it. The fractures in my legs have pretty much healed and, although the casts were supposed to stay on for a couple more weeks, the doctor at the hospital switched to long-leg braces because he felt like it was important for me to start re-learning to walk.

AFTER ABOUT AN HOUR, I've walked the length of four halls, a rectangle around the facility. I'm sure I haven't seen everything, but I'm exhausted, and it's frustrating to be so slow.

"Can we go back now?" I ask Brett, quietly. He's been encouraging and tried to motivate me, but he can tell I'm at my limit.

"Sure. You can have a break, but don't get too comfy. I'll be back in about an hour to take you to the gym." He smiles, and I'm pretty sure I'm not imagining the little gleam that shines off of his teeth. I grin more to myself than to him because in my head, I hear the little *ding* that should go with the gleam. Either he doesn't notice, though, or he's cutting me some slack, because he doesn't bug me about it.

Once back in my room, Dad decides *he* should annoy me instead.

"He seems like a nice young man, doesn't he?"

"I guess."

"Well, he seems to like you and it looked like you like him, too."

"Seriously, Dad? God. You know I'm not interested in anyone but Cal. Brett *seems* ok, at least when he's not being egotistical."

"I thought he was just being positive and encouraging. Maybe he'll rub off on you," he chuckles.

"Yeah...don't get your hopes up."

Brett explained that he will be my primary therapist but that he is an intern working under the supervision of a physical therapist whose name I already forgot. I guess that's why he looks so young. During our walk, I noticed that many of the other patients are old. I did see a couple of people who looked like they might be a little older than me, but I feel out of place for the most part.

I'm not supposed to be here. This is not how I envisioned my life as a 19-year-old.

Exactly one hour after my walk, Brett is knocking on my half-closed door again. *At least this time he knocked.*

"You ready to work some more?" He asks, opening the door after Dad takes it upon himself to yell for him to come in.

Grimacing, I stand up from the chair by the window that has a nice view of an enclosed courtyard where there are trees, benches and a walking track.

"I guess, but I would like to walk around outside if that's ok."

"Sure, but you have to go to the gym first. We will be doing various strengthening exercises every day. You will actually follow a schedule designed specifically for your needs. Ok?"

"Ok." I don't exactly look forward to exercising my leg, but I do look forward to getting better, so I guess now is as good of time as any.

Dad wants to see the gym, so he accompanies us to the other side of the building.

"Through that door is the pool. You will be doing some of your therapy in there, too, but probably won't start that until next week. We will be assessing you this week so that we can see where you currently are and plan where we want to go."

"A pool will be nice, huh Sera?" Dad chimes in.

Nodding, it brings about the first real smile on my face. I always loved swimming in our backyard pool, especially at night with only the underwater light on. The glow of the moon and stars relaxed me. Floating on my back, I would look up and think about my Mom being in heaven, and about how the whole, huge world could look up and see the same sky. It was a sense of connection.

"Hey...Sera, where did you go?" Brett asks, noticing I've stopped by the door to the pool and am staring off into space.

"Sorry; I was just thinking. Let's go."

"Don't worry. Like I said, you will get to spend plenty of time in the pool soon enough," he says, thinking he knows what I was thinking.

And while I'm excited about that, my thoughts had actually progressed to Cal. Even though we are far away from each other right now, I definitely still feel connected to him. I just hope he will wait for me.

NOW

$41.20 in tips. Not bad for a first day of waitressing. I have to be back at the diner by 10:30, which leaves me an hour and a half.

Setting my alarm, I fall back onto my bed and decide to give myself twenty more minutes of sleep.

I'M TAKING the long route to work, slowly passing Cal's shop. I want to stop. I really do, but I feel so nervous. I didn't see him anyway when I *inconspicuously* looked out of my peripheral vision. It's almost like I'm starting all over again, but this time I'm even less confident than the last time.

"HI MANDY. Are you working the day shift today?" I ask her.

"Yeah. Marge called in sick, which is kind of weird. She never calls in. I hope she's ok."

"Me, too."

Other than work-related conversation, we don't get a chance to talk again until around 4:00 with the lunch crowd lasting through early afternoon. We have to take turns with our breaks, but since it's not busy, Mandy stands on the other side of the counter where I sit at the bar. It's the first time I've sat down all day, and my knee is definitely tired. Popping three ibuprofen with my Diet Dr. Pepper, Mandy asks me the inevitable.

"So, what happened to your leg anyway?"

I try so hard not to cringe. I can't avoid talking about it forever; and, while it's nobody's business, I realize it's normal for people to wonder. Plus, Mandy seems like a nice girl, and I wouldn't mind getting to know her since I could use a friend.

"I was in an accident. I've been in the hospital and rehab for the last eight months," I say, looking at my wringing hands. Mandy is a couple of years older than me I think.

"Wow, that's awful. So, you're ok now I guess?"

"Yeah, for the most part. I'm supposed to be continuing rehab, but I moved, so for now, I just plan to work and maybe eventually I will go to college. How about you? How long have you worked here?"

"About six months. I'm working my way through college. I live here in town with my aunt and her family. Otherwise I would have to commute about an hour each way where my parents and little sister live."

"Awesome. I was planning to take some time off from school after graduating last year even though I had been accepted into Baylor. My dad wanted me to go there, and I kind of did, too, but then I met my boyfriend. We had plans to travel for a year before going to school."

"Awww, so what happened?"

"He was with me when we had the accident. My dad had me flown to Dallas, and my boyfriend stayed here. I actually came back to find him. I haven't talked to him in so long."

"Wow. That's crazy. Your boyfriend didn't visit you in the hospital?"

"No, but I'm not sure if Dad really told him where I was. So, I kind of left without telling my dad where I was going and came back here to find my boyfriend."

"That's so cool. I bet he will be so happy to see you again."

"Yeah, I hope so. I'm really nervous though since I haven't seen him in forever."

"I'm sure it'll be fine," she says, but the conversation is interrupted by a group of guys all wearing camouflage who are excitedly discussing hunting while Mandy puts a couple of tables together for them. I grab the silverware and menus to help her.

And it doesn't slow down again until closing.

WALKING UP TO THE TWO-STORIED, grandiose house the following morning, I knock on the assuming wooden door before me. It never intimidated me before, but today I don't feel like Chasity's world is my own anymore. Before I lose my nerve and turn to leave, the large door opens and I'm greeted by Chasity's mom.

"Oh my goodness, Sera! I didn't know you were back! How are you doing?"

"I'm doing well. Is Chasity here?"

"Well no, honey. She's gone off to school in Austin. University of Texas. Remember?"

"Oh, yes. Of course. I just wasn't thinking," I tell her, trying to make up for my mistake. I hadn't even thought about the fact that she would be gone, that she wasn't involved in the same hell as me. "I'm sorry. Could you just let her know I'm back in town if she comes back to visit or something?"

"Of course, Sera. I'm sure she'll be glad to see you again," she says, looking back into her living room, telling someone she will be right there. I guess she has friends over or something. Clearly distracted by her more *important* guests, she seems disinterested in me anymore.

"Ok. Thanks. I'll let you get back to what you were doing," I say, and before I can even make it halfway to my car, she's already shut the door.

I feel disappointed. And I question all of the relationships I've ever had. Chasity is gone, her mom obviously never really cared about me, and I have no friends except for Mandy, who I've only known for two days. I just don't know if I can handle it if Cal rejects me, too.

When did everything change? Was it when my mom died? When I met Cal? Or am I just now, finally, opening my eyes to reality? With the ability to see more clearly.

Walls that divide.

But which side of the wall is good? Deception weaves a golden web, falsely creating an illusion of happiness.

CHAPTER 22

BEFORE

C onflicted.

Two weeks undergoing intense physical therapy, mostly with Brett, I feel confused and unsure of my path. Each day passing creates further separation from my previous goals. Who I was and who I am now.

Dad has backed off. He can't spend every moment with me right now, partly because I'm busy, but also because he's busy. I think his relationship with my stepmom has become a priority, its neglect finally catching up. I'm cool with it. I don't need my father here every second hovering over me.

Brett has been kind. And I don't know if that's good or bad. Obviously, I don't want my therapist to be cruel, but I feel guilty every time I notice little things. Like, when he massages my legs before manipulating them for various exercises. Shame overrides pleasure, tension the victor.

"Just relax," he tells me, gently rubbing my calves before working up to my knees and my lower thighs. With my braces off, I almost feel normal, if only for a moment.

My long hair is pulled up into a high, messy bun, and my workout attire allows for flexibility. But relaxing? I'm struggling today. "I'm trying," I tell him, unconvincingly. "Can we just move on to whatever's next?"

"We can, but you will see more progress if we can work out this tension."

"Ok," I agree, looking up at him. Making eye contact, he continues to rub my legs, so I look down again, frustrated at the blush I feel burning my face accompanied then by a small grin. It's embarrassing. I call it my funeral smile, the one that pops up at inappropriate times and suggests inaccurate and misleading feelings. *Oh God.*

"See, it's not so bad, is it?" he asks, smiling back.

Following my funeral smile, the ugly counterpart, which I call my foot-in-mouth disorder, proclaims, "Umm, I have a boyfriend."

Really? Why would I tell him that right now? It's not like he's flirting with me. He's doing his freaking job. I chastise myself, trying not to shake my head revealing I'm an open book.

His response is unexpected, though. With a cute little smirk, he asks, "Oh yeah? Where is he?"

"What do you mean, where is he?" I ask, feeling immediately defensive.

"Well, you've been here for two weeks, and this is the first I've heard of him. So, where is he?"

"God, you really are irritating. He doesn't live here. Ok?" I don't want to let him win by telling him anything more than that.

"Ok. Then I guess I have nothing to worry about, huh?" I can't read him very well.

"I didn't say you did. I was just making conversation," I tell him lamely.

After that *lovely* encounter, I think he's more touchy-feely than he was before, and again, I'm really not sure how I feel about that.

"I have to stay late today. How about I bring you something for dinner so you get a break from the cafeteria? I could bring some checkers or something. But I'll warn you now, I'm good."

"First of all, you really are full of yourself," I tease him. "And secondly, is my therapist allowed to bring me dinner?"

"Yes, and yes." He answers, grinning back at me.

Rolling my eyes, I give in. "Fine, but FYI, I can kick your ass at checkers any day."

THANKFULLY, Brett has maintained his distance. I'm enjoying his company, but I would never betray Cal. I tell myself that I just need a friend. It doesn't matter that he's my physical therapist, or that he's a super cute guy. *Right?*

"Dude! I told you I'd kick your ass." I tell him after beating him for a third time in a row.

"I'm letting you win, you know," he says, chuckling. He's changed into jeans and a t-shirt.

"Yeah, right. You should stick to your day job." I joke. "Seriously, though, thank you for coming tonight. It gets really boring around here."

"I can imagine. I haven't seen anyone but your Dad visit. What's up with that? There's no way a girl like you has no friends."

"A girl like me?" I ask for clarification.

"You know, a cheater at checkers."

"Ha ha. You crack yourself up, huh?"

"Yep." He looks down for a minute before becoming a little more serious. "Actually, I meant a girl like you who is pretty, funny, a hard worker. There should be a line out the door of people waiting to hang out with you."

"Ok. That's a little overkill, don't you think?" I say, trying to dismiss the *pretty* part.

"Nope. I'm serious. You are my favorite client."

"Whatever. That's because the rest of your clients are, like, a hundred years old."

He laughs. "True, but you would still be my favorite." He grabs my hand, but only holds it a moment before I pull away, guilt once again consuming me.

"I'm sorry. I can't do this."

"Sera. I really like you. But I'll stop. Ok? I would never want you to feel uncomfortable," he says, his hands up in surrender.

"It's ok. I like you, too. I just...I'm serious with my boyfriend. He was in the accident with me, and I haven't been able to talk to him since then. I don't know why he hasn't come to see me. My dad didn't approve of us, and I'm afraid he's keeping us apart."

"Why didn't your dad approve of y'all?"

"Because Cal wasn't like us. He didn't have money, or a big house, or whatever it was that Dad thought made a person good."

"Your dad seems to love you, Sera. I'm sure he was just doing what he thought was best. Either way, for right now, you need to focus on yourself, on getting a hundred percent better. You have your whole life ahead of you and you can't let an accident hold you back."

"Yeah..." The silly mood in the room has dissipated, and I'm ready to be alone for the rest of the night.

"Listen. How about this? I can be your physical therapist by day and your friend by night. There's no harm in being friends, right?"

"Sure," I say, forcing a small smile on my face. Brett has definitely gone out of his way to help me. I don't want to hurt his feelings, and I do appreciate him. "Sounds like a good plan. I had fun tonight, and that hasn't happened in a really long time," I confess.

"Good." He gets up to leave. Hesitating, he pulls me into a hug. "Don't stress, Sera. Just let me be here for you. K?"

I nod, at a loss for further words for tonight.

Conflicted.

NOW

"How are things going?" Mr. Woodward asks. Outwardly, his gruff appearance and initial standoffishness are a façade for the kind-hearted man he is on the inside. I remember feeling a little leery of him the first time I met him in the Red Hawk Cabins office. But every day, he greets me when I see him on the property, usually working on something.

"I'm doing great today, Mr. Woodward. How are you?" I've worked until 5:00 and am expecting Mandy to come hang out a little later. She's bringing pizza.

"Doing fine. The wife dropped some more cookies by for ya. They're up in the office if you want to go get them."

"How nice. You have both been so gracious these past two weeks. I love it here."

"Well, if you need anything at all, we're right here."

"Thank you," I say, smiling as I head to the office to get the cookies. She has left other treats for me so I'm excited. It's almost like having grandparents. My dad's parents died before I was born, and my mom's parents both passed when I was little, so I've never had that kind of relationship, at least that I can remember. Mr. and Mrs. Woodward make me feel safe, both so genuine and thoughtful.

Mandy arrives shortly after I've returned to my small but cozy cabin.

"Hey girl!"

"Hey! I'm so glad you could come." It's the best feeling to have a friend, someone I can trust.

"This is an interesting place to live. I almost didn't find the place."

"Yeah. I remembered seeing it once when I was with my boyfriend. Anyway, it's kind of out of the city and I like that. I know my dad will be around town looking for me before too long."

"You can't hide from him forever, you know." She says, gently.

"I know. Here, hand me the pizza and I'll show you around real quickly before we go inside."

Taking the pizza in, I regroup.

"Do you miss your parents, Mandy?" I ask her.

"Sometimes, I guess. We were pretty close, but it was too quiet at my house. I worry about my sister. She has to be bored out of her mind. Why? Do you miss your Dad?"

"I do, but I don't miss his controlling me. He meant well I guess, but God, he was keeping me from everything I wanted in life. I felt so trapped. Here, I feel free; it's such a relief."

"I can imagine. My parents weren't really controlling, but they definitely had rules. At my aunt's house, things are a little more laid back, but obviously I can't just go wild or they would probably kick me out. I would love to have a place of my own like you do."

"That's the only thing about this place. I just rented it for a month, and I have two weeks left to figure out what to do next."

"Oh man, that's gonna go by fast. I'll help you as much as I can. I have some friends from school who live in an apartment complex in town. It seems like a pretty nice place."

"Awesome. Maybe you could go with me to check it out."

The lake is calm today, a breeze gently swaying the trees and brush around it. The weather here has always been crazy, cold one day and warm the next despite the winter season. Today it's around seventy degrees, perfect for short sleeves and jeans, but near the lake, a light jacket would be more comfortable. Since neither of us have one, we decide to go inside to hang out.

"What's up with the t-shirt hanging on the wall?" she asks, giggling.

"Oh. Let me introduce you." Removing the t-shirt, the old, ugly fish stares at us, causing Mandy to laugh. "I haven't named him, but he's so sweet looking, huh?" I ask, sarcastically.

"Definitely. He's freaking looking at us though, like he's some kind of pervert fish. Ewww, cover him back up."

Now we are both cracking up, trying to hide his thirty-year-old scales and beady eyes.

"So, tell me more about this boyfriend of yours. Do you know where he lives?" Mandy asks.

"No. I know he lives with his Mom, or at least he did. Oh my gosh, Mandy. What if he left town without me? We had planned to go travel the United States. I've driven by the shop where he used to work several times but he's never there." I have worried about how he will react when I find him, but I hadn't thought about his not even being here until just now. "He's partly the reason I wanted to work at the diner. We were going to meet there one time, so I kind of hoped maybe he would come in eventually."

"Hmmm, what does he look like? What's his name?"

"His name is Cal. He has brown hair, a dimple on his right cheek when he smiles. I don't know. He's just really hot. He's kind of quiet, though, at least until he gets to know you. God, I really miss him."

"He sounds great, Sera, but there are a ton of guys around here that meet that description," she says, giggling. "I mean, holy cow, girl, at school, there are a ton of hot guys!"

I realize we've only been talking about me and my situation. "Do you have a boyfriend, or anyone you like right now?" I ask her.

"Meh. There's one guy who I think is cute but I don't really know him. He's in my art class and he always hangs out with this blind guy. Speaking of him, you should totally come with me to my art show. That blind guy is seriously gifted. I've never talked to him, but he sculpted these angels last semester that were so pretty. I have no idea how he does it. I mean, they are way better than anything I could do and I can see."

"Wow. That's so interesting. I would love to come with you. Just having a place to go sounds fun right now. So, are you majoring in art?"

"No. I'm just taking the classes for fun. I'm majoring in English, but I had to take two semesters of fine arts, and I thought those classes would be cool."

"Hmm. I'm terrible at that kind of stuff, but it does sound fun. I still have no idea what I want to do with my life. I feel like it's been put on hold." I confess.

"You'll figure it out. Maybe you should take some classes next year. You could save up your money."

"Maybe... I still hope I can find Cal first. I know I can't plan my whole life around him exactly, but I just don't want to do anything or make plans until I at least know how he feels about me. I love him, Mandy. I know it sounds dumb, but seriously, it was like love at first sight, at least for me," I add, dreamily.

"You're young, Sera. It could be love, but just know that no matter what, you have to keep moving forward. I had a boyfriend in high school. We dated for two years and then all of a sudden, he had to move away, and we kind of quit talking. After, like, three months, we both decided to break up. And I'm not trying to discourage you. I just don't want you to get your hopes up and build all of your dreams around someone you haven't seen in a while. Ya know?" She is trying to be gentle, and I appreciate that we can talk, but I refuse to give up hope, at least in my heart. For now, I simply nod in agreement.

CHAPTER 23

BEFORE

Pool therapy is my favorite by far. Gliding through the warm water doesn't feel like work; in fact, it's extremely relaxing. On Mondays, Wednesdays, and Fridays, I attend strengthening classes, which are actually pretty fun. The older patients are sweet. Watching them dance along with the music inspires me, puts things into perspective. There is one old couple, Arnie and Edith, who attend together. They are apparently outpatient because I only see them during class, but I've talked to them a few times. Married for 60 years, they still hold hands, their love evident each time their eyes meet. It's beautiful.

Brett works with me in the pool on Tuesdays and Thursdays.

"Ok. Let's continue to work on range of motion today," Brett instructs. Sometimes he has me walk on an underwater treadmill, but today, he's in the water with me.

My hair is put up in a high ponytail, and I'm wearing a bathing suit that I ordered online. It's a purple, white, and black tankini with a cropped top and boy shorts for the bottoms. I love how it covers me but still looks flattering. After the accident, I lost about eight pounds. I was never big to begin with, but at a size 9, I always felt much larger than my size 0 friends. Now, a size 7 boosts my confidence a little in my new suit. While I realize it shouldn't matter, I can't help but want to look cute.

Flexing my knee is so much easier in the water than in the gym, but it still hurts, the grimace on my face betraying my attempt at maintaining a brave face.

"You alright? Here, let me help you," he says, noticing. With one hand on my thigh pushing downward, he uses his other hand to gently push my calf up. I can't extend it all the way or bend it very far yet.

"Ok, ok, ok. Just be careful," I say, breathing through the pain.

"Ok. You're fine. Just relax and let's push it as far as it will go. I don't want you to be in serious pain, but you do need to push yourself."

After about twelve reps, I get to take a break before the next set.

"So, did you get a new bathing suit?" Brett asks me. I had been wearing a one-piece that didn't fit well and he knew how much I hated it because I complained several times about it.

"Yes," I tell him, smiling.

"Looks nice. And I like this," he says, pointing to a small tattoo that is peeking out from the suit bottom on the inside of my right hip.

"Oh, crap. I didn't realize it was showing. My dad doesn't know about it, so please don't tell him. Ok?"

"Sure. What is it?"

"It's a little red heart locket." I don't tell him the story behind it.

"What does this one mean?" I ask Cal, lying on the couch after making love. My fingers trace the gold wings extending out from behind a grayscale skull with a red rose beneath it. The tattoo on Cal's chest is quite beautiful and sexy as hell, I might add.

"It represents freedom," he tells me, caressing my hair. "I can't

wait to get on my bike and just ride. You and me; we will see it the world. It's gonna be fucking amazing."

"As long as I'm with you," I add. "And this one?" I ask, touching his bicep where a tiger looks like it's crawling up to his shoulder.

"Ha, that was my first one. I just thought it looked cool," he says, chuckling.

"It looks good, very realistic, if you could actually have a little tiger crawling up your arm," I say, laughing with him.

Before I can examine the others, Cal silences my questions with his mouth on mine, kissing me deeply. "God, I love you," he whispers.

"I love you, too," I profess while looking into his eyes.

"You never judge me. I know you're better than me, but you don't care that I have tattoos, that I'm different."

"Of course I don't care. Cal, if you could see what I see, maybe you would understand. I mean, yeah, I think you're super freaking hot, but you are truly beautiful. It's who you are. I've never had someone care about me like you do. I trust you completely."

He pulls my head to his chest and kisses my head, embracing me. "You are beautiful, Sera. There's no comparison."

"Thank you. Hey, would you take me to get a tattoo, too? Like, soon?"

"Seriously? I'd love to take you. The guy who has done mine is pretty good. Let me see if he's free anytime soon," he says, getting his phone out to text. "What do you want to get?"

"I'm not sure. Do you have any ideas? Are you going to get another one, too?"

"I could. Hell, I wouldn't mind getting a new one every week. Once you get one, it's hard to not want to go back and get more every chance you get."

"I'm thinking I should start out small, like maybe something here," I say, pointing to the inside of my right hip right above my panty line. "I need to be able to keep it covered so my Dad doesn't see it. I don't want to give him any reason whatsoever to freak out."

"*Mmm, so sexy,*" he says, touching the spot tenderly. "*Sounds like a good plan,*" he agrees. "*How about we get tattoos that go together, something that will mean something to us. I want you to always remember me when you look at it. Like, maybe you could get a heart locket, and I could get a key. I've seen different ones together, but it would be cool to each have part of it.*"

Bringing my hand to my mouth, I exclaim, "Oh my God, babe. That sounds perfect." I can't help the tears in my eyes; I'm so moved and happy.

With his thumb, he wipes my eyes while cradling my face in his large, strong hands.

He is my safety and my freedom. I can't wait to spend every moment of my life with him.

"Hmm, it's sexy. I would have never had you pegged to have a tattoo," Brett tells me, breaking my memory. And I'm back to reality, my dreams suspended in *recovery.*

"Thanks, I guess."

"It's a compliment. Why are you all of a sudden down?"

"I'm ok. I was just thinking about my boyfriend. Sorry." While I'm flattered by his attention, I don't want to lead him on. No one will ever be a substitute for Cal. He's permanently etched on my skin, and in my heart.

"Ok, let's go ahead and get you on the treadmill for the remaining thirty minutes." Changing the subject abruptly, I'm afraid I've offended him. But gosh, just because he's cute, I'm not going to fall all over him. I don't even acknowledge him as I walk through the water to the end of the pool where there is another section with treadmills. Honestly, I need a break from his flirting.

NOW

"What should I wear to your art show on Friday?" I ask Mandy.

"Do you have anything that's nice but not too dressy?" she asks me.

"Nothing that I really like or that fits me well. I mostly brought casual clothes since I couldn't pack everything. Plus, most of my clothes are too big right now."

"You wanna go shopping? It would be fun," she says, singing out the word, "fun."

Clapping my hands like the overenthusiastic dork that I am, I jump up and down and squeal. "Yes! I haven't been shopping in forever, and I haven't wanted to go by myself. Are you off tonight?"

"No. I have to work until close. How about tomorrow? We could go after work then."

"Yes. I'm off at 5 tomorrow. I'm so excited. I love new clothes," I tell her.

"Me, too."

THE KNOCK on my door has to be Mandy. Nobody else knows where I'm staying.

"Just a second," I yell, heading to unlock and open the door while putting my other earring in. I haven't even really fixed up in forever. The little black dress I found when I was shopping with Mandy is sexy but not too risqué. Falling about mid-thigh, the sleeveless, fitted fabric with a lace overlay has a plunging v-neck in the back. It's the only part about which I feel self-conscious, but Mandy insisted I get it. Opening the door wide, Mandy steps in.

Whistling, she yells, "Girl, you look hot!"

"Thank you. Are you sure it's not too short?"

"No. I mean, yes." Laughing, she adds, "You know what I mean! Really, you look great!"

"Dude, you look great, too!"

Twirling, she responds, "Thanks!" She's not lacking in confidence, which makes me laugh, but I'm thankful for her friendship because she helps me come out of my shell.

I can't wear heels yet. Having been clumsy before the accident, my balance has definitely not improved since. Sometimes it's disappointing, but at least I found some cute, strappy sandals that look good with the dress. They are black and silver, and they tie in nicely with the silver jewelry I found to match it.

"You would think we were headed to a club instead of an art show," I say, laughing.

"I told you there are hot guys at my school. We can't go looking all crappy, you know."

"True. It's kind of fun getting all dressed up anyway."

"It is. Now, let's get out of here." Mandy drives a black Mustang. The leather seats and new features are so fancy compared to my old Bronco. I love my car, but Mandy's is super nice.

"I love your car, Mandy."

"Thanks. It was my graduation gift."

"Wow. How nice!"

"Yeah, I love it, and I'm definitely thankful, but my parents don't give nice things without strings attached. I will be glad when I can get out from under them."

"I can understand that."

WALKING IN TOGETHER, I try to borrow some of Mandy's confidence. She notices me wringing my hands.

"Dude, chill out. It's only an art show."

"I know," I say, giggling. "But I haven't gone out in a long time, and I think this dress is all of a sudden shorter," I add, tugging at the bottom.

"No, it's fine, so leave it alone. Just come on ya big dork. Pretend you are going to a museum."

Laughing more, I tell her, "I haven't been to a museum since my third grade field trip, and I wouldn't have worn this dress in third grade."

"I'm seriously gonna have to get you out more," she says, cracking up.

Entering the glass double doors of the Civic Center, we follow the small crowd to one of the larger event rooms.

"Why is this here instead of at the college?" I ask her.

"Because it is a show for the city and surrounding areas. Our work will be exhibited, but there will be different kinds of art from all around here."

"Oh wow. That's cool."

People mingle around the large room filled with paintings, sculptures, drawings, woven rugs, jewelry, among other various art forms.

"Come on. I get extra credit for being here, so before we look around, I want to see if I can find my teacher to let him know I came," Mandy says, pulling me.

"Ok."

One large section appears to include multiple projects from the school, identified by a sign in a metal stand. Mandy stops to talk to her instructor while I wander off. She catches up with me as I near the collection of sculptures.

"Where is yours?" I ask her.

"Right there," she says, pointing to a small clay figure, clearly molded into some type of bird.

"What is it?" I tease her.

"Shut the hell up. Obviously, it's a bird," she giggles. "I told you I'm no expert."

"No. I was just teasing. I like it," I tell her. There are probably twenty different projects lined up against the wall on a long cloth-covered table. Each has a framed title and artist card identifying the work.

"Look at this one, though," Mandy tells me, pulling me to a separate round table centered in the room, as if to showcase it.

Turning around, I stop completely, before walking slowly to inspect it closer. The clay sculpture is larger than the others and extremely beautiful. A large heart stained red with intricate designs and a keyhole in the center stands about six inches off of the table, suspended in the air with metal wires that create an almost invisible stand. Attached to the heart is a golden key with a clay chain, but one of the links in the middle of the chain appears to be broken. The entire sculpture appears weathered, as if it's ancient, but the spotlight shining on it reveals its true beauty. Breathless, my eyes become glassy, my hand coming to cover my own heart.

"Oh my God," I whisper.

Noting my reaction, Mandy responds, "I know. It's gorgeous, isn't it?"

Nodding, I feel a loss for words, but I'm looking for the little card identifying the artist.

"Mandy, who made this?" I ask her, thinking it's surely a coincidence.

"That blind guy that I was telling you about that's in my class," she says.

"But..."

And then I feel it. Flickers of hope, of love. Sparks, as if a lighter is almost out of fluid, the flint still devoted, still hanging on. Heat fills my body, consuming my thoughts. It's like everything in the room disappears, the white noise surrounding me, background for a single moment. Turning around, I see him standing across the room accompanied by a guide dog. Sunglasses mask his face, but I can feel him.

"Mandy, what is his name?"

"Whose?"

"The guy who created this."

"Oh, umm, Chris, or Curt...something like that? Why?"

"Cal?" I whisper.

"That sounds right. Why are you...? Oh my God, Sera. Cal? *Your* Cal?" She asks, realizing suddenly.

"What should I do?" I feel like I'm going to freak out. Partly because he's here, within steps from me, but partly because I never thought about how he was affected by the accident. Shocked and sad, I have my hand over my mouth, taking it all in.

"Talk to him." She encourages me.

But before I can decide anything, he's walking towards me. It looks like he is staring right at me, but he can't see, right?

Stopping a step away from me, he tests me.

"What do you see in this sculpture?"

Does he sense it's me? Oh my God.

"Us?" I whisper, questioning. Confirming.

And his head falls, tears streaming down his cheeks.

"Cal?" I don't know what to say.

"It can't be," he says.

"What?"

"You. You were gone. I don't understand," he says, wiping the tears. "She said you were gone."

"Who said I was gone?"

"My mom. I asked about you, but she said you were gone. Oh God, Sera. I thought you were..." he says, clearly unable to continue, to say it out loud.

"My dad...he took me to a hospital in Dallas. I've been there ever since. But I came back. To find you."

"Great. And look what you found. I'm broken Sera. As you can probably tell by looking at me. I mean, I can't be who I was anymore. I can't even take care of myself, much less you. You need to find someone who is better for you."

"Are you kidding me, Cal?" My raised voice draws unwanted attention so I lower it. "We are both broken Cal. God, I've been through hell. My legs were broken; I had a shattered knee; I've been through multiple surgeries and rehab. It's been horrible, but I'm here now."

"I'm sorry. I wish I never would have taken you on my bike. I'm so sorry, Sera."

"I'm not angry with you, Cal. Can we just go talk somewhere?"

"I don't know. It's like, I couldn't stand the thought that you were gone, that I caused it, but now, I'm afraid I can't be the man you need."

"Cal," I say, grabbing his hand.

He squeezes it for one minute before letting go, the tears escaping beneath his dark glasses once again, and he turns to leave. And I'm not broken anymore.

I'm shattered.

CHAPTER 24

BEFORE

"Dad, Brett told me himself. He thinks I'm ready, that I can just come in as outpatient."

"Yeah, but I want to make sure the doctor and the physical therapist in charge agree. Ok?"

"Is there some reason you don't want me to come home?" I ask him.

"Of course not, honey. You know I want to spend as much time with you as I can, but I don't want to rush anything."

I've followed Dad to the main office where we are waiting on the small loveseat on the other side of the secretary's desk. Near it is a living room area, kind of a common area for patients that is not too far from the cafeteria. The rooms are only separated by a half-wall to allow for an open concept.

While waiting to see the director, I grab Brett as he is walking by.

"Can you please talk to my dad? He doesn't believe I'm ready to be discharged."

Shaking my father's hand, he begins a conversation. Because I'm so frustrated, I decide to sit in the nearby living area. Hopefully, Dad will listen to Brett if I'm not involved. It's when they lower their voices that my interest is piqued. Without making it obvious, I walk towards the window that leads to the courtyard because it's a little closer, within hearing distance.

"Why did you tell her she's ready? We discussed this when she was admitted," I hear my father say.

"Because she is. She doesn't need to be here anymore, and we both know it."

"But I'm not seeing *progress*."

"Yeah, she's shut me down every time. It's not gonna happen, sir," Brett says, sounding frustrated.

What in the freaking hell?

"Well, then I guess you can tell your grant goodbye, huh?"

My father doesn't continue to wait to talk to anyone else but instead briskly walks to me and tells me to start packing.

And I am livid. Not because I'm leaving, because believe me, I'm more than ready, but because my father, *and* Brett, have obviously betrayed my trust, yet again. Disgusted, I can't even make eye contact with my father. I haven't decided whether or not to confront him either, because right now, all I can think about is getting far away from here. From everything.

IT'S VERY STRANGE ENTERING my house considering I've never lived in it before. Dad told me he moved and bought a home here, but it feels wrong. My room is full of boxes. My belongings packed by someone other than me. Infected. With the poison of untruth. Loyalty and honesty compromised, running through the veins of a home belonging to someone else.

My father's narrow-minded master plan is selfish.

I can forgive him, eventually. But his ironic plan to keep me close pushes me further and further away.

NOW

"Please take me home," I tell Mandy. She stood witness to the conversation I had with Cal.

"Ok," she says, softly. "Let's go."

Where do I go from here? I can't go back to living with my father, as his pawn. I just can't. And I still want to talk to Cal, but I can't exactly force him to listen. To keep loving me.

With one week left in the cabin, I have never felt so conflicted and confused in my entire life.

"It's all going to be ok," Mandy assures me. She didn't want to leave me alone, so I loaned her some pajama pants and a t-shirt so she can stay the night with me.

"I don't know, Mandy. I really don't see how anything is ever going to be ok again. And I can see how you think I'm being overly dramatic, but what would you do? I mean, my father is *not* an option, and God, Cal..." My tears take place of words. Burying my head in my pillow, I scream. I'm sad. Frustrated. Angry. "It's just not fair. I worked so hard to get back. To me and to him, and he just pretty much dumped me."

"Ok. Just calm down. You have to think about the fact that Cal just found out you are here, *and* that you are alive. How awful that he thought you were dead all of this time! He's probably shocked. Give him some time. I'm sure he will come around."

"Maybe. But what do I do in the meantime? I can't hide out in this cabin forever."

"Let's go look at the apartments I was telling you about tomorrow. Ok? And then we can figure things out, but we don't have to do it all tonight. Try to look on the bright side. At least you found him."

"Ok. I'm not giving up yet. I can't let him go that easily, at least without talking to him some more. Thank you for being here for me. You are the only one I have right now."

Mandy's hug provides comfort. For the moment.

~

IN AN OLDER PART OF TOWN, the apartment complex surrounded by large oak trees sits nestled near a park, its old Mission architecture a beautiful contrast to the greenery and flowers. Despite the age, the neighborhood seems very safe.

"Would you like to see one-, or two-bedroom units?" the apartment manager asks.

"How much are they?" I ask her, thinking the price will influence my decision more than anything.

"Well, the single units are $400 per month, and the doubles rent for $700," she informs me, passing brochures to Mandy and me.

"Thank you," I tell her. Looking at the floor-plan for the one-bedroom, I begin to get excited about having a more permanent, temporary home. "It looks nice, doesn't it?" I check to get Mandy's opinion.

"They look great if you ask me." She's looking at the two-bedroom floor-plan. The sparkle in her eye suggests she's got a plan.

"What would you think about having a roommate? If we split the rent, it would be cheaper than if you rented a single unit, and I would enjoy having a place of my own instead of living with my aunt's family."

"That would be really awesome actually. Are you serious?" I ask her, the excitement contagious.

"Yes," she says, giggling.

"Could you show us a two-bedroom? Do you have any available right now?" I ask the lady.

"Actually, you're in luck. One just became available last week, and it's already cleaned with fresh paint, ready to go. Would you like to take a look right now?"

"Yes," both Mandy and I say in unison, laughing.

The 600-square-foot apartment is simple, but perfect. Tile floors meet carpet between the small kitchen/dining area and the living room. Two bedrooms down a short hall are separated by a good-sized bathroom with a linen closet and hall closet. Each bedroom has windows that overlook the park and small walk-in closets. The kitchen appliances are old, but it doesn't matter. We both love it immediately, already planning where we will put our few belongings.

"You're absolutely sure about this, right?" I ask Mandy.

"Definitely!" She answers.

"We'll take it then!" I tell the manager.

"Great," she responds. "Let's go fill out the paperwork and then we can get your keys and go over all of the terms and conditions."

Mandy and I hug and proceed to follow the lady while she takes us the long way back to the office, pointing out a pool and hot tub enclosed by a black iron fence. The whole complex is charming. Finally, something good brightens my mood.

After an hour and a half, we have the keys to our new apartment. Because we both have to hurry to work, we decide we will have to wait a day to move in.

Mr. and Mrs. Woodward told me to come visit them before leaving. They stand waving goodbye as I drive away, the gravel in their parking lot kicking up with the roll of my tires onto the smoother pavement. A smoother road ahead.

Mandy's aunt has an extra couch and end table, as well as some kitchen stuff: pots, pans, dishes and silverware. It's enough for the two of us and a couple extra in case we ever have visitors. Her aunt even gave Mandy the bed she's been using while staying with them. I, however, do not have a bed, so we head to Target to get everything we need. Settling for a futon, I grab some extra throw pillows and sheets with a blanket to serve as a bed. With cute, retro blue and white fabric, it will come in handy in case I ever use it as a couch. I've never been good at making my bed in the mornings though, so I figure it will usually be covered by the blue, purple, and white patterned comforter and sheet set I purchase.

After buying a microwave, a gray and green chevron shower curtain that we both like, and a few groceries, we are set until we can save more money to add where we need it.

Since I haven't needed to spend much from the money I've made working, I've saved around $500, which added to the money I had before, brings me back to just over $1000. It's too much to carry in cash, but getting a bank account makes me a bit nervous. I'm still not ready for Dad to find me, even if I'm getting out and about a little more.

One perk of working at the diner is that Mandy and I are able to eat for free while we are working as long as we do it during our break. I like to have a bowl of cereal in the mornings and have found that I can survive on Ramen noodles for dinner when needed, so our grocery bill shouldn't be too excessive, not counting the staples: Diet Dr. Pepper and some kind of candy. Both are a must.

Since I didn't have siblings, the opportunity to share my space is new but inviting. Mandy and I get along well; she's my best friend.

CHAPTER 25

BEFORE

"I don't want to see Brett anymore," I express adamantly to Dad on the way back to therapy. Home for a week, my first appointment for outpatient care comes too quickly.

"Why not? He took great care of you for over a month."

Still keeping my knowledge of their conversation secret, I am forced to make up a reason. "There was a different physical therapist there, a girl named Rosy, who I really liked. She filled in sometimes, and I can relate to her."

"We'll see."

I'm way too old for 'we'll see.' I think.

Unfortunately, Rosy is not working today, and Brett seems ever too eager to continue where he's left off.

"You seem quiet today," he notices.

"Yeah, I just want to keep working. I'm ready to be done with all of this."

"Well, just because you changed to outpatient, you still have quite a rough road ahead of you; so, while I want you to stay positive, you also need to realize that full recovery takes time and patience."

"Ok." My short answers get under his skin, evident in his irritated expression.

Foolish Brett. It's not about him, so he can suck it. The dang smirk on my face reveals my sarcastic thoughts, so I try to disguise them by taking a few slow, deep breaths through the exercises.

"Good, good. I think you are well-stretched and warmed up. Let's move on to do some wall squats."

"I could do these at home, you know, if you just want to teach me a few more so that I will have a routine."

"I can teach you some at-home exercises, but there are some you need to do under our care and with the equipment we have here. Ok? Are you trying to get rid of me?" he asks, chuckling.

"Yep," I answer candidly. I laugh with him so that he can't be sure whether or not I'm joking. Always so careful to be polite, I've never allowed this side of me to come out. It's kind of fun to be a jerk, especially when it isn't too obvious. I'm tired of being stepped on, run over, controlled. I won't be a puppet ever again.

"Well, how was it?" Dad asks on the way to the house.

"Oh, you know, great as always," I say, smiling while looking out the window, such a small piece of glass separating me from the real world.

"That's good." I'm not sure if he recognizes my sarcasm and just doesn't want to confront me about it, or if he really is that clueless. I'm hoping for the latter. Maybe it will make for an easier break when the time comes.

"You know, I was thinking, maybe you should go ahead and start some online classes this fall. I know you aren't ready to be on campus, but nothing has changed since you were accepted to Baylor."

"I don't know, Dad. Maybe I will wait until Spring. I'm just not quite ready yet, ok?"

"That's fine, Sera. You take the time you need. Just don't let too much time go; I don't want you to lose your dream," my father says.

When did he lose sight of who I am? Of my dreams? I'm not even sure what my long-term dreams are. Especially now.

NOW

While Marge isn't exactly the typical mother figure, her support and encouragement comfort and embolden me. It's as though I've gained a whole new family here: grandparents, a mother, a sister.

"Thank you for helping me, Marge. I had no clue what I was doing."

"You're welcome, sweetie. Sometimes we have to learn as we go. It's not easy being a grown up, you know."

"Yeah, I'm sure I could have eventually figured them out, but filling out forms for financial aid was definitely overwhelming."

"I understand. Honestly, it was easier for me because I helped my niece with the same thing just last year. She's attending a small college up in the Panhandle."

"That's cool. I'm not absolutely positive I will start anytime soon, but Mandy insisted I need to get the FAFSA filled out right now just in case."

"It's hard to know what you want to do in life when you are your age. It will come though. Don't be like me; working at a diner at age 60 is not easy. I mean, don't get me wrong, I love the people here, but my body is tired," she explains.

"Thank you. I hope I'll figure it out before it's not too late."

"Oh, you will, honey. You will."

Working an extra shift tonight to help out and also to make a little extra on my paycheck, I get my flexible knee brace out of the Bronco.

I keep it in there for times like this. I'm supposed to wear it all the time, but I don't feel like I need it unless I'm on my feet all day.

Mandy had the earlier part of the day off since she had class today, but she's working with me tonight.

Thankfully, she arrives early, which gives me a chance to grab a bite to eat before the rush. Sitting on my usual bar stool, Mandy sits next to me, also eating. Marge will still be here for thirty minutes, and there is only one table of two in the diner at the moment.

"Hey, so I had art class today."

"Umm, you seriously don't need to tell me about it, Mandy."

"I know, but I thought you might want to know that Cal came up to me and asked me about you. I guess Ray, his friend, saw me leave with you the other night. Ray is that cute guy I was telling you about. You know, the one I kind of like?"

"Yes. So what did he ask you?" On the edge of my seat, I'm dying to know anything and everything about the boy I fell in love with, the boy who has changed so much in the last nine months. I don't care that he's blind. I mean, I care about his feelings, and that it has to be so hard for him, but not for my own sake. I wish he understood that.

"Well, anyway, Ray," she continues with a dreamy look in her eyes, "led Cal over to where I sit on the other side of the room. I hadn't ever talked to Ray so I was super excited that he came over, that he knows who I am."

"Oh my gosh, Mandy. Seriously? Stop keeping me waiting or I'm gonna have to totally kick your butt!" I say, giggling.

Laughing with me, she adds, "Alright, alright. I'm getting there. Just chill."

I swear, she's keeping me in suspense like some ridiculous reality show where the judge has to wait what seems like for-freaking-ever to announce results. I *hate* that.

I give her a *look*, so she finally spits it out, "Ok, so Cal asked me if I was your friend and if I knew where you are."

"Yes?" I ask, dragging out the word while waiting for more.

"Yes, and so I told him."

"What?!? What do you mean you told him?"

"Well, I figured it would be fine to tell him. I just told him that we recently moved into an apartment together, and I *might* have told him that you work here with me."

"Oh my gosh, girl. What if he comes in here? I look like total crap after working all day!"

"Dude, he can't see you anyway."

Gasping, I tell her, "Stop. You are such a butt. But I do kind of love you right now," I say, grinning widely.

"Of course you do. I'm pretty amazing," she replies, laughing.

"Yeah, yeah. You're just using me to get to Ray, huh? So did you also tell *him* where we live. Huh?"

"You know I did. I even suggested he and Cal come visit sometime."

"Holy crap. You are so crazy. I'm never that brave, but I'm glad that you are. We make a good team."

"Ha. And which part of the team are you, Sera?" she asks.

"The pretty one of course," I tease her. She smacks my arm before getting up to get her apron. A family of six just arrived. I guess I better get back to work.

Feeling giddy, I clean tables and serve people with a huge smile on my face all evening, but the only one who comes through that door that I care about is Mr. Jordan. I've served him every night that I'm here since working at the diner. With the same picture of his wife on the opposite side of his table every single night, he has begun to open up to me, sharing a bit of his own story.

"It's good to see you smiling, Sera," he says, sitting down slowly, removing his hat.

"Thank you, Mr. Jordan. It's been a pretty good day today."

"What's different?"

"Well, I fell in love with this boy last year, but I haven't seen him in a long time until the other night. I wasn't sure that he felt the same anymore, but he indicated that he might come talk to me, so I feel happy about that." Something about Mr. Jordan makes it so easy to confide in him. His wise eyes are always understanding.

"Aha. I've sensed something like that about you. Do you remember when I told you that you are a fighter?"

"Yes, sir."

"Well, you need to fight for that love, for that boy. You know, if Mrs. Jordan wouldn't have fought for me, I wouldn't be sitting here today."

"Really? What happened?"

"We met when she was 17. I'm 5 years older than her, so I was 22. I was in Wisconsin training to be an airplane mechanic after enlisting in the air force, and one Sunday, at a church off base, I saw her sitting there next to her parents on a pew a few rows in front of me. Her long, red curls fell down her back all the way past the back of the pew. She was absolutely stunning. I guess she could feel me staring because all of a sudden, she turned back and smiled the most beautiful smile I've ever seen. I tried to return the smile, but I think I was frozen in place."

"Aww, I love this story. So, did you talk to her after church that day?"

"Nope. I had to make it a whole week before seeing her again, but you better believe I was at that church every Sunday for the next four weeks just to get a glimpse, to experience that feeling that I'd never felt before her. After a month of going but never speaking to her, I learned that I would be transferring to a base in New Mexico within the next month. I figured I might never get the chance again, so I went up to her and her parents after church that day and asked if I could take her on a date to get to know her. Her parents balked at the idea, so she wasn't able to agree that day, but her wink and smile when she was leaving gave me hope."

He's looking at the photo on his table, remembering.

"So then what? How did you get the girl?"

"Well, her parents didn't think I was the one I guess, so I gave up. I never wanted to cause conflict for her. But the week before I had to leave, she told her parents that she loved me, and that she planned to marry me. She told me this later. I couldn't believe she loved me when we hadn't spoken much. I'd never even told her how I felt yet. Anyway, my transfer got postponed for one month, so we spent every moment possible together. After three weeks, despite the fast courtship, we got married, finally receiving her parents' blessings. We moved to New Mexico together a week later; and, while we had our ups and downs, we were together for 60 years. When I would worry about money, she would always say we were rich in love." His eyes mist with the memories of his love, and mine tear up as well.

"What a beautiful story, Mr. Jordan. I can only hope to experience a love like that."

"You will, Sera. I sense it for you. You just keep hanging on; don't let go no matter what."

Although Cal didn't show up that night, the disappointment I felt was overshadowed by hope. Hope for long-lasting love.

And I would wait if I had to.

CHAPTER 26

BEFORE

A ll alone in my dad's new house, I decide to look around. I've always enjoyed treasure hunting shows, where people find things where they would least expect it; so, when I climb up to the attic, it's exciting to see a bunch of boxes and other things.

Pulling the cord hanging above me, light illuminates the room full of treasure. What surprises me though, is that the treasure is my own. Pieces of my past, of my childhood, of my mother. Things I never knew existed.

A large trunk occupies a corner by a small window. The intriguing space captivates me. Sitting on the small stool next to it, I open the trunk to find what looks like my mother's belongings.

Gasping, I whisper, "Oh my God."

Her wedding dress wrapped in plastic lies on top, so I hold it out to better view it. The vintage lace covering the bodice boasts gorgeous beadwork with a satin gown that flows to the ground, a long train following behind. With a button back, it's so beautiful. I can't believe I've never seen it. It looks like this dress has been passed down from generation to generation.

I drape it over some of the nearby boxes so that I can inspect the other contents of the trunk.

An old doll, a small trinket box holding costume jewelry, and what looks like school items rest on one side, letters and cards on the other. Handling them gently, I finger the items carefully, feeling a connection to my mom that brings tears to my eyes, but the letters are what seduce me. I don't know how much longer Dad will be gone, so I take the letters to my room after carefully returning the dress to the trunk. Not sure of the reason for the secrets, I don't want Dad to know I've been rummaging through everything.

MOTHER's DAY cards from me to my mom lie on top of the stack. Homemade, they are cutout hearts decorated with glitter, the elementary handwriting expressing my love for her. Despite the twelve years that have passed since she passed, the feelings are fresh. I miss her terribly. There are three, each from different years, and one has my kindergarten picture on it. I had just lost my first tooth in the picture and my sun-kissed brown hair was curled with a ridiculously large pink bow on top of my head. Giggling, I think, *oh well, I guess I worked that giant bow.*

The letters appear to be from my father to my mother.

Dear Gwen ,

Do you know how much I love you?

I'm so glad we were able to spend time together last night. I know your parents are worried, but they don't need to be because I promise you, I will do whatever it takes to earn their trust. I can take care of you. I can work during the day and go to school at night. I'll work two or three jobs if I have to. You and the baby mean everything to me, and there is nothing in this world that will keep me away from you.

I know you wanted their approval, but I think getting married is still the right thing to do, and I cannot wait until this weekend, when you will officially be my wife. I love you so much, babe, and I promise I will give you the world.

Please don't be scared. Just trust me. I will pick you up on Friday night like we planned.

Love always,

Henry

MY PARENTS never told me that I was conceived before they married, or that my mother's parents didn't want them to get married. Dad has been pressuring me to go to college since I was in junior high. I don't remember his going to school; as far as I can remember, my father worked as a stock trader. We never lacked for money and were, in fact, considered well-off, so the revelation this letter provides shocks me.

I find my Dad downstairs, having heard him come in about thirty minutes before.

"Dad, please don't be mad, but I found something that I want to talk to you about."

"Ok..." he says, slowly. "What is it?"

"Well, I was bored and I was looking around and I found the pull string for the attic door. Anyway, I went up there, and I looked inside a big trunk. Why have you never shown me Mom's wedding dress?"

"I was waiting until you are older and ready to get married, Sera. What else did you look at?" He seems a little angry and nervous.

"The letters. I read them, Dad."

"Honey, that's personal. I wish you wouldn't have done that."

"Whatever, Dad. You read my freaking diary, or do you not remember that? God, Dad, *why* have you never told me the story of you and Mom? That you got her pregnant before getting married and that Grandma and Grandpa were unhappy about it? You've always led me to believe you did everything right, Dad."

"Sera, I think I did do everything right, for the most part. I definitely don't regret having you. Your mother was scared, but she was so thrilled to find out she was pregnant. We loved each other."

"Then why are you so against Cal and me? Seems a little hypocritical if you ask me," I gripe.

"Because I want the best for you. You need to go to college before settling down with someone. You are young; and, even though I wouldn't change it now, I don't want you to have to go through the struggles your mother and I had. Cal didn't even know what he wanted to do after graduation, Sera. You're going to Baylor. I don't want him to hinder you. If you still care about each other after college, then you can explore a relationship, assuming he does something with himself. But I can't stand by and watch you make a huge mistake without trying to protect you, even if I have to protect you from yourself. Plus, look at what that boy did to you. My God, Sera, you would have already been in college and never had to deal with all of the pain and trials concerning your injuries if it weren't for him. He almost killed you, Sera," my father says, getting louder with each word.

"Dad, I chose to get on that bike with him, and it wasn't his fault anyway. I love him. Why can't you see that? I don't have to do everything according to your plan. This is *my* life, not yours," I yell back.

"Sera, you are young. I know you care about him, but just wait until you are older to find love. Let me help you go to college, get settled in a career, and then maybe the timing will come."

"I'm not giving him up, Dad, no matter how hard you try to keep us separated."

"We don't need to continue to discuss this, honey. You need to stay here and finish recovery. If he is still around waiting for you after that, then fine. But he's a young man. He may have moved on already and you need to accept that. Ok?"

"God, Dad. Thanks for being so encouraging. You're right. I don't need to discuss this with you anymore," I tell him sarcastically, thinking he doesn't need to know what I'm thinking.

NOW

It's been two days since Cal asked Mandy about me. I kept hoping he would stop by the diner so we could talk, but...*nothing*. Feeling disappointed, I decide to try not to think about it.

Because we always have a large crowd for breakfast on Saturdays, I've been working since 8:00 this morning. Exhausted, I have to sit down for a break at 5:00, right as Mandy arrives for her shift to relieve me.

"It's been a crazy day today, non-stop," I inform her.

"Ugh. I hope it calms down some. My legs are sore from working out yesterday. As long as nobody drops something, I'll be fine. It hurts to bend down," she says groaning and laughing at the same time.

"Join the club! My legs get so tired after a full day like today. I was running back and forth, back and forth. I had a table of 12 that stayed forever after they were finished eating. They were nice, but they were all chatting and just hanging out while I continued to refill tea and coffee. I finally got to sit down a couple of minutes ago, thank God."

"Well, I can take over from here so you can go home and chill," she says, smiling.

The bell on the glass door dings, alerting us of more customers coming in.

Mandy smacks my arm suddenly and scream whispers, "Oh my gosh, they're here!"

"Ow." Rubbing my arm, I turn to see who she's talking about and immediately freak out when Cal and Ray are walking into the diner. Ray says something to Cal, and he looks in my direction.

"I've got this," Mandy says before walking to them and seating them in an end booth that is more out of the way. She comes back to me, telling me, "I sat them in my section over there so hopefully it will be a little quieter. They asked for you, so go over and sit with them."

"Come with me. My feet don't want to move because I'm so nervous," I plead.

"Ok, fine, but then I have to get to work. Ok? I'll check on y'all as frequently as I can though."

The butterflies in my stomach feel more like bats, fluttering gone crazy.

"Hi," I say, timidly before joining them. Ray is sitting on the opposite side, so I sit next to Cal.

Breathing him in, I recognize the soap he used before. He smells so good.

"Are you smelling me?" he asks, grinning.

"What? No." I lie.

"I heard you. It sounded like you smelled me when you sat down."

I'm thankful he can't see me blush, but that lasts for about two seconds when Ray decides to enter in to the conversation.

"I think you must be right, Cal. She's blushing."

"Dude!" I object, giving him a look that he better recognize before I die of embarrassment.

Cal chuckles, the sound such a reward that I decide it was worth it. "So, how have you been?" he asks me.

"Good. Umm, I'm living back here again. Like I told you, Dad took me to Dallas for treatment, but I left and came back. How about you? I really loved the sculpture you created. It was so beautiful. I had no idea you are so artistic," I compliment him.

"Thanks. I'm doing ok, especially right at this moment," he tells me, flirting. He angles his body to better face me, causing his knee to touch my thigh. I swear I feel the heat from that one spot spread throughout me. His jeans and black fitted t-shirt look so incredibly hot with his brown, messy hair.

And his lips. I've always loved the shape of his lips. I want to put my fingers on them. Kiss them. But I snap back to reality.

"Me, too." I concur. "Thank you for coming to talk to me."

"Yeah, I'm sorry about the other day. I was so surprised, and you would think I would have handled it differently, but I think I just didn't know what to do or think. As you can see, I lost my sight as a result of our accident. It pretty much sucks. God, what I wouldn't give to be able to see you right now."

I feel so horrible for him. I really can't imagine what he's going through.

The adrenaline rush, a result of our meeting, gives me the courage I need to touch him. Grabbing his hand, I rub my thumb over the top in a reassuring manner. His head lowers at the touch, and he visibly looks pained and relieved at the same time, his audible sigh confirmation.

Ray mentions, "Yeah, I had to kick his ass a little. This douchebag has been mopey ever since I met him, and then I find out that you are here and he told you to go. What the hell, man? I was like, 'Hell no! You are going to fix this, ya fucking dumbass.'" Cal chuckles next to me, and the vibration moves through our hands.

Oh God. I just want to hug him, or maybe straddle him, but that would be super inappropriate.

"It didn't take me long to realize I was a fool, anyway. God, Sera. I hate that we lost all of this time. I don't even know how you feel right now, but I want to get to know you all over again. I want to find our way back to each other, if you think that's possible."

"I want that, too, Cal. You have been my motivation for getting better this whole time. I've missed you every second of every day."

On that note, Ray decides to give us some privacy, getting up to walk over and sit at the counter. Mandy immediately meets him there. She only has one other table to tend to at the moment, so hopefully they can get to know each other.

"So, where's your dog? He was beautiful."

"I decided not to bring him tonight since Ray is with me. I have a cane that I have learned to use pretty well so I brought it instead. I've only run into a *couple* of buildings," he jokes. "Luke is great, though."

Giggling, I say, "I had to use a cane for a long time, too. It's great fun."

"Are you ok now, Sera? I can't tell you how horrible I have felt ever since the accident. God, I'm just so thankful you are here."

"But your mom told you I was gone? I don't understand."

"Yeah. I asked her about it after talking to you the other night. I was very angry with her at first, but I think she was just trying to protect me. I guess when she realized I misunderstood, she didn't want to correct me because she wasn't sure you would ever come back. Apparently, your dad saw her after the accident and told her to keep me away from you."

"Oh my God, Cal. That's terrible. I can't believe all of the ridiculous and awful things he's done. I've told him over and over that I would find you. I had to sneak out. Left while he was at work. Can you believe he actually bought a new house in Dallas? So yeah, I drove all the way here by myself."

"And I'm so glad you did. If I could just talk to your Dad...well, I don't know. He will probably discourage us even more when he realizes I'm..." His head drops again, this time in defeat.

"Cal, stop. I don't care what my dad thinks. I mean, I love him and I know he loves me, but he doesn't control me anymore. Ok?" I ask, worried that he will leave again. "Besides, you said you would never leave me. Remember? And I'm gonna freaking hold you to it this time!"

He raises his hand to touch my face, so I lean into it, soaking in the warmth and strength, an extension of who he is. I cover his hand with mine and turn to kiss it. Before I know it, he's leaning into me.

"Come here," he whispers, intimately.

Our foreheads touch, and it reminds me of the time we spent at the park once. We can't exactly be affectionate in the diner, but at least we are able to connect like this.

"When I realized I couldn't see anymore, I was devastated; I'll admit. But, it was losing you that really hurt. You were my light, Sera, and the darkness surrounding me for the last nine months has been suffocating me. I can't ride anymore. I can't travel the US like we wanted to do. I didn't plan on going to school either but my therapist suggested it, and honestly, sculpting has given me a small outlet for my grief. You have been my muse, babe," he tells me, smiling.

"I'm so sorry you had to go through all of that, Cal. I've missed you more than I can say."

His lips brush mine softly before he backs away so that we can continue to talk. It's a kiss I can feel throughout my body, causing an urgency to pick up where we left off. Cal recognizes my desire.

"Holy fuck, Sera. I'm dying here. Change the subject or something," he says, shifting in the seat.

"Ok," I answer, giggling.

CHAPTER 27

BEFORE

"I really don't need to go to rehab anymore, Dad. I can do the same things at home." Trying to convince him is useless but I can't help but try. After hearing Dad and Brett talking, I can't stand the thought of seeing Brett. It's funny how someone can be so attractive physically, yet disappointingly ugly on the inside.

"You're going, Sera. I don't want to argue about this with you."

Sheesh. He's especially grouchy today. I guess he's taking a different tactic for controlling me. He obviously doesn't want to even give me a chance for freedom. Of any kind. Quickly jumping out of the car, I don't even tell him *goodbye*. His mood is contagious. Or maybe it was the other way around. I don't know and I don't care.

Brett's fraudulent smile deters my own.

"You know, you need to work on that attitude of yours, Sera. Seems like you've reverted back to the negativity consuming you when you first got here."

"Seriously, Brett? Has it occurred to you that maybe you are the reason for my *attitude?*"

"What the hell did *I* do?" he asks, sounding incredulous.

"*You* were collaborating with my Dad, weren't you? I heard you. I know there was something going on. Did he hire you to be my physical therapist? Why don't you clue me in?"

"I don't know what you heard, Sera, but no, your father did not hire me to work with you. I advocated for you. Your dad wanted you to stay longer, not me."

"Then what the hell was he saying about you not getting some kind of grant?"

Sighing, he opens up a bit more. "Ok. He didn't hire me, but he did promise me he would fund a large grant for our facility if you and I ended up together."

"What?! You can't be serious." Shocked and angry, I want to hit something.

"It's not what you think though. Stop," he says, trying to calm me down while I'm furiously pacing. "Just listen for a minute, will you?"

My foot pointed outward with my hand on my hip, I can't even look at him, but I stop to listen to what he has to say. He takes a minute to compose himself before explaining, "Ok. The thing is, I'm really attracted to you, and your Dad kind of noticed that when you first got here."

"How did he notice?"

Shaking his head, he can't help but smile when he continues. "So, I was checking you out one day while you were walking ahead of me. He pulled me aside and asked me if I had feelings for you, so I said, 'yes,' because I did, Sera. I do. But you keep talking about your boyfriend all the time, and I guess I just figured it wasn't gonna happen."

"I've been very upfront with you about that, Brett. I'm sorry, but I can't change the fact that I love my boyfriend."

Interrupting me, he adds, "Yeah, a boyfriend who isn't here. I'm here, Sera. *I* am. I know you feel something for me. Your blush gives you away."

"Cal's probably not here because my freaking dad is trying to keep me away from him. I just know he brought me to Dallas for *that* reason more than for anything else."

"Your Dad obviously loves you. I'm sure he would never try to hurt you. If he really is trying to keep you away from your boyfriend, maybe he has a good reason."

"Oh my God, Brett. You just don't get it. I mean, of course my dad loves me, but he's a control freak. He's practically holding me captive. It's ridiculous. And whatever his reason is, it sucks. Because I'm smart enough to choose who I love," I say.

"You're right, and I'm sorry. Ok? Will you forgive me so we can just move forward? I genuinely do want the best for you. I want to help you recover completely; and, if your boyfriend doesn't come through, will you consider at least one date with me?"

Although I still feel frustrated, it's nice to know that Brett isn't as bad as I was beginning to think he was. The thought of his helping me while having ulterior motives disgusted me.

"Fine, but don't count on me coming back, because once I'm back with my boyfriend, I know everything will fall back into place. Thank you, though, for telling me the truth. I appreciate that, and I'm thankful for your help."

Nodding his head in response, we spend the next hour working my legs. It's probably the most relaxed I've felt in a session so far.

BACK AT THE HOUSE, Dad suggests I unpack the boxes that remain piled up in my room. Because I don't want him to become suspicious, I decide to go ahead and unpack at least a few. It bothers me to place my beloved things in this room, so I try to focus more on clothes and things that have less meaning.

This will never be my home.

NOW

"What else is on the list?" Mandy asks me. We are shopping for tonight. Cal and Ray are coming to our apartment, and we are both so stinkin' excited.

"Let's see. We need to get a chair or two, and I was thinking we might want to get some snacks. You have to buy the beer since I can't. Oh, and a birthday cake!" I say in a singsong voice.

"No. We do not need a cake," Mandy insists.

"Yes, we do, and we're getting one whether you like it or not," I tell her.

"Dude, the guys don't know it's my birthday, and I don't want to make them feel weird."

"Whatever. We're getting a cake," I assert, "*And* candles!"

Huffing loudly, she smiles. "Fine, you win."

"You know I do," I tease.

CARRYING TWO PIZZAS, the guys stand waiting at our doorstep after ringing the doorbell. Mandy is still touching up her makeup, so I answer.

"Hi, y'all. Come in," I invite them, smiling. "Why don't you just put the pizza on the counter in the kitchen, and we can sit in the living room while we wait for Mandy."

Taking Cal's hand, I lead him to the loveseat that we found online. It's used, but it looks new, the leather in perfect condition. We couldn't pass up such a great deal, and we had planned to buy a couple of chairs anyway.

The weather is unseasonably warm, so I am wearing shorts and a t-shirt, choosing to be comfy since we are just hanging out in our apartment. Sitting next to Cal, I tuck my feet beneath me so that I can face him. His hand naturally falls to his side and finds my leg, so he caresses it, making circles with his thumb. Such a simple action stirs up my emotions.

"I've missed you," I tell him.

"Me, too."

"Can I hug you?" I ask, feeling a bit nervous and unsure.

Holding his arms out, he welcomes me to him and pulls me close, practically up onto his lap. My arms hug him tightly over his shoulders, his around my middle, embracing for several minutes before Ray finally clears his throat telling us to get a room.

I'm thankful to spend time with Ray and Mandy here, and I initially thought it would be good to have a buffer, but surprisingly, I feel so comfortable with Cal, like the last nine or ten months never happened. Before he lets me go, he whispers into my ear, "Later. I fucking promise." I'm sure he hears my sigh in response. I have to force myself to be quiet, the involuntary groan almost escaping.

As I break apart from his embrace, he grabs me, his arm around me keeping us as close as we can be. God, I can't even explain the intensity of being wrapped up at his side. So good. Safe, free, forever.

When Mandy finally comes in wearing a cute, casual dress, I can tell she is definitely hoping for something more with Ray, and looking at his expression when he sees her, the feeling is clearly mutual.

Cal jokes, "I know I can't see what's going on, but damn, I sure can feel it. It's not just *us* who need to get a room." Giggling at his teasing, Mandy comes over and announces, "I'm gonna punch you now, just so you're ready," before punching him on the arm. He and Ray are both laughing, the mood for the beginning of our night fantastic.

After we eat pizza and talk for a while, Mandy and Ray decide to go for a walk outside. Since there is a park across the street, they plan to go hang out on the swings.

"It's about time," Cal says.

"Seriously," I agree, hoping we can spend some time catching up in a more intimate way.

"God, I wish I could see your beautiful face, Sera. In my mind, I can, but I know it's not a true substitute. But I can smell you, hear you, feel you, and that's more than I ever thought I could have again."

"It's ok to touch me, I mean, if you want to."

Without further words, his hand moves to my face. He touches my cheeks, my chin, runs the pads of his fingers over my eyes and nose, and then his fingers thread through my hair, pulling me to him, his mouth taking charge as it envelops mine.

"Mmmm, you feel so good, Sera. Your hair is like silk, so soft." He kisses my eyelids, my cheeks, and then shifts down to my neck.

The heat in the room rises hastily, matching our belated desire.

My hands snake around his neck, playing with his messy hair, duplicating his touch. "Please stay with me forever, Cal," I whisper, shivering beneath his trembling hands.

"Baby, I just got you back. I will never let you go again. I'm just afraid this is all a dream," he confesses.

When I pinch his arm, he jumps. "What the hell?" he asks, clearly at a loss.

"I'm just proving to you that this is not a dream," I explain, giggling.

"Oh really? Remind me to get you back for that later," he says, chuckling.

The Bluetooth speaker Mandy and I recently bought softly plays in the background following a playlist from Cal's phone since I haven't added music to my phone yet.

"Is this the playlist I made for you?" I ask him.

"It is. I listen to it every day."

"Awww. That's so nice. I need to see if we can somehow get it on my phone, too."

"Ray is pretty good with that kind of stuff. We can ask him later," he tells me.

When one of our favorite slow songs comes on, I ask him to dance with me.

"I can't dance, Sera. I'm less coordinated now than I used to be, and even then I couldn't dance," he says, smiling.

"Come on. Just stand up and hold me. We can sway to the music."

Pulling him up by his hand, he takes me into his arms, the rhythm naturally leading our movements.

The flutter between us is arousing a blaze.

THE COOL AIR swishing in with the opening of the door alerts us to Ray and Mandy's return. *That* in addition to their out-of-breath laughter.

"Oh my gosh. A cold front is moving in or something. The wind is crazy, and it's all of a sudden freezing out there," Mandy explains. "I told you I would beat you," she chides Ray, to which he replies, "Yeah, because I gave you a head start."

Hand-in-hand, apparently their walk brought them closer.

Cal and I are quiet, the interruption probably good before we were consumed.

After another hour of chatting and forcing Mandy to blow out her birthday candles while we sing obnoxiously loudly, the guys have to leave.

"I really wish you didn't have to go," I tell Cal, my arms wrapped tightly around his waist. "Me either. When can we get together again? I need to prepare my mind because, right now, it's fighting me, telling me to never leave your side."

"Ummm, well, I have to work tomorrow until close, but I get off at 5:00 the day after that. Any chance we could hang out then?"

"It may be more like 6:00 before I'm able, but that works for me. What do you want to do? Want me to come here again?"

"Let me double-check with Mandy and make sure she doesn't have anything going on, and I will let you know. Do you text? I mean, can you? Or do you just want to call me?" We exchanged numbers the night he came to the diner.

"You can text me because I'm able to listen to it, but just know that when I speak to text, it's like autocorrect gone wild. Ray cracks up at some of the weird shit I end up sending him, so sometimes it's easier to just call. Plus, I want to hear your voice instead of the phone voice anyway."

"Ok, we can talk tomorrow. I miss you already," I say, feeling down before he even leaves.

"I love you, Sera. I'm so incredibly thankful for you, and I will do whatever it takes to be with you, so just hang on, because if we could get through the hell we've already gone through, we can get through one more day. Ok, babe?"

Standing on my tip-toes, I pull him down to kiss his lips. "I love you, too, Cal. See you soon."

CHAPTER 28

BEFORE

Megan, my stepmom, is only ten years older than me. She's obviously never been like a mom to me but more like a babysitter. I don't dislike her, but we've never been close. I don't even think my father is that close to her. He changed after my mom passed away. The fear of losing someone immediately replaced grief, winding through his thoughts like weeds strangling new growth. But instead of keeping her close like he does with me, he keeps his distance, and I think she resents me for it.

If she could only understand that I don't want him to smother me like he does, maybe she wouldn't appear overly needy to him, which seems to push him further away.

It's not my job to facilitate their marriage, but if he could transfer his need to hold on to me, perhaps the weeds would loosen their grip, providing freedom for their relationship to flourish.

I'm planning to leave in one month, just after Christmas, so I have thirty days to bring them closer together, not for her, but for him.

And for me.

I love my dad. He makes me angry sometimes, but I don't want to leave him while he feels so out of control that he tries harder to control everything around him. While I realize I can't change him, I hope to give him an opportunity to relax, especially after he's spent so long helping me with recovery.

"Megan, I was thinking, since I'm home now, why don't you and Dad go out on a date or something? I'm completely fine here without help."

Cleaning the granite counter in the kitchen, she questions my intentions. Small talk here and there is about the extent of our relationship, so I continue, "It's just that, I know my dad has spent a lot of time with me lately, and I think you deserve to spend time together."

"I don't know, Sera. I've been spending more time with my family lately. I hate to tell you this, but I'm not sure how much longer I can handle this. I love your dad with all my heart, but he closes himself off to me. I'm sorry. I know you don't need to hear this right now either. I just feel like you should know."

"Please don't do anything yet." I don't know how much I can trust her not to tell my dad what my plans are, but I wish so badly that I could open up to her, to tell her everything.

"Why, Sera? What's going on? You can talk to me, you know. I know we've never exactly been close, but I do care about you, and I recognize your dad's issues with keeping you close."

Hesitating, I chew on my lip and wring my hands. It's a huge gamble. If she tells him about my plan to leave, he will tighten his grip on me making it more difficult to follow through, but if she hears how I feel and knows what I want to do, maybe she could help me.

Hanging the wet rag on the hook inside the cabinet beneath the kitchen sink, she joins me at the breakfast table where I've been eating a sandwich.

"What is it?" she asks again.

"Well, I don't know what all he's told you, but it's kind of a long story. Do you remember Cal?"

She met him once at the beginning of our relationship, before Dad's reservations became obsessions and prevented us from openly dating.

"Of course. He's a cute boy. Seems really nice."

"Yeah, but Dad doesn't think so. He didn't want us to be together at all."

"I know. I tried to express my opinion about the matter, but he refused to listen. You know your dad, so stubborn," she says smiling. I guess she embraces all of his qualities, even the ones that frustrate the crap out of me.

"Anyway, I don't know if I really *needed* to be transferred here after the accident. I hate living in a big city, and I miss my friends as well as Cal. Plus, Dad has made it near impossible to even connect with any of them. I've tried talking to him, but he cuts me off. Says he's not gonna argue with me. Ugh. I'm just so sick of it," I confide in her.

"Your father loves you very much."

"I know, but don't you agree that he's a bit overprotective?"

Now she looks like the nervous one, afraid to confide in me, so I decide to risk it and tell her everything.

"I love Cal. I really do, and I believe we are supposed to be together. I'm not stupid, though. I mean, I get that we are young, that we haven't been together that long, all of that stuff; but, when I was with him, I'm sure it was real, and I have to go find him. I'm leaving after Christmas, Megan, and please, do not tell Dad. I need a head start before he tries to circumvent the whole thing."

Megan's hesitant response worries me. "Maybe you should just talk to your dad, Sera. If you leave without telling him...Gosh, he will freak out."

"No. I've already tried talking to him. I'm done with that. I was hoping maybe if I told you, that you could help me. Plus, I want y'all to have a chance, and I need to leave for that to work."

Contemplating my argument, she finally nods her head, thinking it all through. "Ok, so what is your plan? Where will you stay when you get there? You know your Dad will find you and try to bring you home."

"This is not my home. Cal is my home, and I don't have everything figured out yet. Honestly, I don't know exactly where he lives or what his number is, but it's a small town, Megan. You know it won't take too long. And it's not just about Cal. I need this. I need to live on my own, to take care of myself."

"I think you are perfectly capable of doing that, Sera. I really do. Let's just think about this though so you will have a better shot at being successful."

"That's exactly why I want y'all to go on a date. You both need it, and hopefully he can shift his focus to you and only you."

Smiling, she is clearly coming around, embracing my idea. "I would definitely like that. You are his daughter, and of course I respect that, but I miss what we had when we first married. I'm scared it's too late, but I'll try one more time. I love him too much to give up yet."

"Yay," I cheer, jumping up to hug her. While it's a bit awkward, I believe it's a great start to a closer relationship to my stepmom.

NOW

Because of both of our schedules, we have been unable to see each other like we had planned, but talking on the phone has been a nightly event.

"Do you realize what today is, Sera?"

"Ummm, Wednesday?"

"Today is the anniversary of when we finally got to hang out for the first time."

"At the park?"

"Yes, when we sat by the little lake at Sullivan Park. You were so beautiful sitting across from me. I'll never forget it. I wanted to fucking take you right then and we hardly knew each other," he says, chuckling.

"Oh my gosh. You are so crazy," I say, laughing.

"I'm serious. Do you know how long I had been waiting to talk to you, to touch you?"

"How long?"

"I noticed you when we first started high school, but it wasn't until we were seniors that I couldn't keep my eyes off of you."

"Why didn't you talk to me sooner then?"

"Because, Sera. You know I was never in your league. I guess I just couldn't stay away from you anyway. You're kind of addicting you know."

Giggling, I respond, "I remember seeing you in the cafeteria looking at me. Oh my God. It was so dang hot. I was like, holy crap, is he looking at me? Lots of girls thought you were sexy, but I definitely never would have thought you would even consider me."

"Why? You're fucking beautiful, Sera. I miss seeing your face. Your gorgeous eyes. I wish I could change what happened to us, but I would never change being with you."

"Me either. I was so scared you would hate me when I finally found you."

"I could never hate you, babe. If anything, you should hate me. It's my fault that this all happened to us."

"No. It wasn't your fault. I mean, honestly, I don't remember much about the accident, but my dad told me a truck hit us after running a red light."

"Yeah, but I should have seen him coming. I'll never forgive myself for not protecting you."

"Babe, please don't do that. If it wasn't for you, I would never know what true love is. You are strong, probably the strongest person I know, and I trust you. Ok? You would never hurt me."

"I don't know about all of that, but I can promise you that I will do my best or die trying."

Tears well up in my eyes. "Thank you, Cal. I love you so much. Now, let's change the subject. No more of this serious talk."

Chuckling, he says, "Ok. How about we talk about how much I want to kiss you right now. I need to touch you."

"Mmmm. Come over, then."

"Oh God, Sera. You know I would if I could. Tomorrow. Ok? I'll get Ray to take me to see you tomorrow night, even if you work."

"Well," I say, drawing out the word, "it just so happens that I get off work at six tomorrow, so I'll be home early. Could you meet me here at, like, seven? I want to have time to shower before you get here so I don't smell like food."

"In that case, I'm getting there at 6:15. Don't start without me."

"Oh my goodness. You are seriously making me hot over here."

"Just wait, Sera. I'll show you fucking hot."

CHAPTER 29

BEFORE

C hristmas décor embellishes the world around me, affectation creating a semblance of happiness. But I'm sure I'm not alone in feeling a lack of complete joy, which is sad because I recognize my blessings. I have a home, a father who loves me, food. It's strange how lonely and sad I feel despite that. I miss home. I miss my mom. I miss Cal.

Regardless, I go through the motions, playing life's game like a marionette, my father's hands manipulating the strings.

"You two sure have been spending a lot of time together lately. It's nice," Dad addresses Megan and me upon entering the living room. We are drinking hot chocolate while wrapping a few presents. Megan's smile is quite lovely. I don't know what took me so long to realize she is a good person. Unfortunately, I've been selfish. I think I subconsciously basked in Dad's attention, the safety net he provided. It was when I met Cal that my vision became clear. Cal is my safety and my future. Dad is supposed to be that for Megan, but guilt steered him wrong, deceived him, inappropriately shifting his focus to be on me.

"We're having fun. Would you like to join us?" I ask.

"I've got to meet with a lawyer regarding your accident in thirty minutes. The man who hit you had insurance, but they are not accommodating us as they should, so I think we will have to pursue further action."

"Oh, wow. Do you know if Cal was compensated?"

"I don't know, honey. Right now, I'm attempting to right a wrong for you."

"Ok. I understand. I hope he has a good lawyer, too," I say, knowing Cal and his mother didn't have the money that we do and how much of a difference that can make, sadly.

Megan muzzles the elephant in the room, changing the subject, "Are we still on for tonight?"

"Yes. Are you sure you don't want to go to dinner with us, Sera?" My dad asks.

"Yep. I'll be just fine here. You two go have fun."

THE WEEKLY APPOINTMENTS at the rehab center have been going well since the candid conversation I had with Brett.

"You are progressing very well, Sera," he tells me.

"Thanks. I've been working on stuff at home, too. When do you think I will be able to stop coming here?" I ask him.

"Well, that's a tough one. You're doing great, but you should continue to utilize our care as long as you are able. Do you find that your knee ever gets stiff, especially in the mornings?"

"Yes, so I've been doing the stretches you taught me. It's at night that it really hurts. My legs feel achy and my knee sometimes feels like it's going to give out completely when I've been walking on it all day."

"That's normal, and it will continue to get better. Let's get you into the whirlpool today since this is a longer session, and then we will follow that with some weight training in the gym."

"Ok. Sounds good."

Since I'm outpatient now, I haven't attended the swimming rehab classes; so, when I enter the pool room, I'm happy to see some familiar faces of the other patients. When I notice Arnie is alone, though, I have to know where his wife is. I wish I would have just asked Brett instead of walking to the poolside and inquiring myself.

"Hi Arnie. Where is Edith today?" I ask him, smiling but with concern.

With tears in his eyes, he answers, "Edith passed away last month."

Shocked and saddened, I immediately apologize. "I'm so sorry, Arnie. She was such a beautiful lady. I enjoyed talking with her during class." My hand is covering my heart. It genuinely hurts for Arnie, and I feel so incredibly sad. Their love was my example, motivation to find *my* other half. In fact, I had mentioned Cal to Edith and she was so sweet. She encouraged me to hurry and get better so I could go back to him.

"The world lost a beautiful soul, but I will see her again. I miss her more than anything, but I know she is safe in heaven, just waiting on me." Tears still gleam in his old, deep-set eyes, but the smile on his face when he thinks of her is touching.

After briefly speaking with some of my other friends, I see that Brett is waiting for me near the whirlpool at the other end of the room.

I was successful at keeping my composure while talking to Arnie, but, once I'm walking over to Brett, I can't help the tears that fall. Tears for Arnie. Tears for me. Tears for all of the bad things that happen to people in this world.

"What's wrong?" Brett asks.

"Oh my God, Brett. Why didn't you tell me about Edith?"

"I didn't know it would upset you. She has been pretty sick for a long time, and she was old."

"But Arnie. How awful for him to be left behind. It's just so sad. I loved watching them in class together."

"Sera, it's part of life."

"But why does it have to be? Why can't they just go together in their sleep or something?"

Brett laughs at that. "Sera, you are such a dreamer. But it's sweet. I love that about you."

The release of crying leaves me feeling a little better. Laughing at Brett's laughing at me makes for a pretty silly session, but it feels good, the tension dissolving somewhat.

NOW

I'm thankful for a slow day at the diner today. There were just enough customers to keep me busy but not too busy. In addition, I'm able to leave right on time, thrilled to see Cal when I get home. I don't know if he was serious about the shower, but I've been thinking about it all day, my face flushing more than once.

Our apartment is only about five minutes away. Since Mandy had the evening shift, we had to take separate cars, so I'm driving home, singing along to the music. The parking for our unit is actually on the back side of the building, our front door opening to a charming courtyard shared with other units, so I park under the carport that lines one side of the parking lot and walk around to unlock my door, totally anticipating a great night.

As soon as I round the corner, my stomach falls when I see my father sitting on the edge of the porch, his long, bent legs a rest for his arms where he is looking down at his intertwined hands. Hearing my gasp, he looks up at me and stands to his feet, waiting, but I've stopped in my tracks, unsure what to do.

"What are you doing here, Dad?" I ask, my voice shaky.

"I've come to take you home, Sera. You've been gone for long enough, and I know you haven't been following up with rehab or your doctors. I tried to give you some time. Megan convinced me to let you go for a while, but God, Sera, I thought you would be more respon-sible than this. I thought surely you would come home after getting this out of your system. You need to go to school, you need..."

Interrupting him, I raise my voice. "Stop, Dad. I *am* responsible. Why can't you ever see the good things? Ever since Mom died, you have lived in fear. Always worried about the worst that can happen."

"And look what happened. The worst did happen, Sera. I almost lost you, and I won't lose you again. Now get your things, and you can ride back with me. I'll send someone to come back and get your car later."

"She's not leaving, sir." All of a sudden, Cal's voice interjects. I hadn't even heard him walk up. Ray dropped him off since Mandy wouldn't be here. He didn't want to be a third wheel.

"Shit," my dad says, looking at Cal. I think his reaction is in part because of Cal's impairment but also because he doesn't want to deal with Cal right now, but cursing is not generally his forte, so the word surprises me.

"*Shit* is right. You're not taking her from me again. I'm sorry, sir, but she's doing great here with me. Look at her. She has a job, an apartment. And she has me. I'm here for her, and I promised her I would never leave her again," Cal says.

"I think you're confused, son. *You* took her from me."

"With all due respect, sir, she's not a little girl anymore. You can't keep her locked up forever," Cal says.

"Yes. I can. I can at least keep her away from you. You are not good for her. Look at you," Dad says, waving his hand towards Cal, raising his voice.

And that's all I can take. I'm furious.

"Stop." I yell. "Just stop." Lowering my voice, I continue. "First, let's take this inside. I don't want to freaking fight out where all of my neighbors can hear it."

Unlocking my door, I escort Cal into my apartment, much to my father's overly loud sigh.

"Ok. Now, everyone needs to chill. Neither of you make my decisions for me. Ok? God. I'm so sick of everyone thinking I need someone to take care of me, like I'm a clueless little kid. I am perfectly capable of taking care of myself. And I think I've done pretty well. Cal's right. I have a job, an apartment, and I even applied to go to school where Cal goes." Before either can talk, I continue, "Plus, I've made new friends, Dad. My roommate, Mandy, has been awesome. She works with me at the diner. And the other people at the diner are there for me, too. There is a lady named Marge who helped me with school stuff. Oh, and when I first got here, I stayed in a place where this really nice older couple were. They are actually like grandparents to me. I have Cal, and we are finally getting to where we were before the accident. So everything is good, Dad. Really good. Ok?"

"Honey, that all sounds nice. But you need to come back so you can go back for doctor appointments and for rehab. We've made a new life in Dallas, Sera. This isn't your home anymore."

"Seriously, Dad? *You* made your life there. Not me. This is my home. Ok? Can't you please just understand that? I can find a doctor here. It's not like I'm living in another country or something. And I can come visit you once and a while, or you and Megan could come here."

Dad's face falls. "Megan left. Last week. Said she felt like I wasn't there for her anymore."

My hand comes to my mouth. "Oh my gosh, Dad. What happened?"

"We were fighting a lot. She said I was too worried about you and that I should let you go and live on your own. I know I haven't been there for her enough, but I had hoped she could forgive me for that. And she knows I've always taken care of you; she needs to let me handle this."

"I agree with Megan," I tell him.

"Then you're both wrong," he says, angry. Back to square one, my dad stands up from his chair while straightening his attire, removing the wrinkles from his plan and from my apartment.

"I'll be back tomorrow, Sera. Get your things together and you *will* ride back with me. I'm already compromising by giving you a little time to say your goodbyes, but *this*," he says, gesturing between Cal and me, "is over." Walking out the door, I am left with no words, and I'm extremely angry.

"What the hell was that?" I ask Cal through gritted teeth.

"That," he answers, "is your dad's unwillingness to lose, but I can tell you right now, Sera, I *won't* lose this fight. You are right where you belong. With me."

CHAPTER 30

BEFORE

"He needs to hear it from you, Sera. Get ready because our appointment is in one hour," my dad informs me regarding a meeting with our lawyer.

"Fine, but I don't want to talk about the accident. I can't remember much about it anyway," I remind him as I walk out of his home office and to my room. Since I've been at home more often than not, my comfortable sweat pants and t-shirt officiate the less than important activities that have become my daily life: reading, sleeping, eating, waiting.

I'm not even sure what the appropriate attire is for a meeting with an attorney, but I decide on black pants with a deep red sweater. My black Mary Janes are old but comfortable and round out the outfit that doesn't accurately portray me at all.

"Don't forget your cane, sweetheart," Dad calls out to me from the garage, keys jiggling in his hand.

"I don't need it if we aren't going to be walking far, Dad," I explain as I near the car.

"Get it. I want him to see what you've been going through."

"God, Dad. Seriously?"

"Yes. Hurry up."

Frustrated, I return inside to get my cane, taking my time as I casually make my way back to the garage. It might be just a little passive aggressive, but it's the only control I have, so I'm taking it.

Rolling his eyes, Dad clearly recognizes my antics and doesn't comment, as if he's not willing to stoop to my level. We drive in silence until we are parking in a downtown parking garage. As the barrier gate lifts, Dad takes a slip from the machine that states the time we arrive.

Making conversation, he explains, "We will get this validated when we leave. Are you nervous? You haven't said a word the whole way here."

"A little. I just want to get this over with," I tell him, annoyed with the whole process. I want the man who hit us to be held responsible, but I don't know to what extent, and I wish it could be done without my involvement, however unrealistic that might be.

THE DECORATIVE CHANDELIER hanging overhead reflects brightly on the center of the long mahogany table stretching the entire length of the rectangle boardroom, a wall of windows boasting a beautiful view twenty stories into the downtown Dallas skyline. Cold air blows down directly on me. How do I always pick the coldest spot in a room?

Rubbing my arms, I wait alongside my father for the attorney to come into the intimidating room.

After about ten minutes, a man who appears to be in his 40s briskly steps into the room, firmly shaking hands with each of us before taking the seat at the head of the table next to my father.

"Hello. I'm Davis Cole. It's nice to meet you both." Looking at some notes on a legal pad, he appears to familiarize himself with our case for a moment while we wait silently for him to continue the conversation.

"Ok. I spoke briefly with your father, but I need to ask you a few questions, Sera."

I quietly respond with a simple, "Ok," anticipating the difficulty of the subject matter.

"I understand you were in an accident. Tell me everything you can remember about it."

Sighing, I wring my hands as I try to gather my thoughts. "Umm, well, I can't really remember much about the accident itself. The last thing I remember is that we were going to my boyfriend's house to study."

"Ok. And your boyfriend, he was the driver?"

"Yes, Sir. Cal is his name."

"Where did you meet Cal?"

"At school. Why?"

"I just have to gather as much information as possible, Sera. I need to get the big picture in order to represent you effectively. Now, how long have you known Cal?"

"Ummm, we started talking about four months before the accident."

"Ok. Was Cal under the influence of anything that day? Did he ever use illegal drugs, prescription drugs, alcohol during the time that you knew him?"

Feeling defensive, I sigh and speak in frustration. "No. He didn't use anything. He wasn't some kind of thug."

"I'm not attacking his character, Sera. These are things I need to know."

"Ok. I'm sorry. I'll do my best to answer whatever questions you have." I can't even look at my father. I already know how he felt about Cal, and I can't help but wonder if he told the attorney that Cal was bad. Plus, Dad didn't know I was with Cal when the accident happened, so that makes this more uncomfortable. Megan let me go with him that day because I knew that Dad would have never let me go, especially since he didn't even want us dating.

While I would love to have this conversation with the attorney in private, I'm pretty sure Dad would freak out if I asked him to leave, so I guess I will have to do the best I can. Clasping my hands in my lap, I take a deep breath and try to relax.

"Why don't you tell me more about Cal? What's he like? How old is he? Does he live with his parents? That sort of thing."

"He's great," I say, a huge smile taking over my face. "Cal is kind, funny, smart, handsome. He lived with his mom. His dad apparently left before he was born. He doesn't have any siblings. He was... not wealthy." I look down, annoyed that I have to describe him that way. "His mom worked a lot and he also worked, at a gas station as a mechanic."

Dad grumbles beside me, interrupting me: "He got in a fight with my good friend's son, and he took Sera on that stupid motorcycle after I made it clear that it probably wasn't safe. I saw the tattoos he had. I don't think he was as perfect as Sera thought."

"Stop, Dad. God, just stop. You didn't even know him. He fought Chance because Chance attacked him for no reason. And he was a safe driver on his motorcycle. He even bought me my own helmet. He would never, ever hurt me. And his tattoos do not make him bad. Ok? God. I don't know why you can't at least try to accept how I feel about him. You haven't even let me see him or call him since the accident, Dad."

Mr. Cole interjects, "Ok, ok. We aren't here to put Cal on trial. Right? We are just establishing fault, and right now, it doesn't sound to me like Cal was at fault for the accident. Quite frankly, Henry, that's a good thing. We don't want to make him look like a bad guy, regardless of your perception of him."

Dad sighs next to me, and I feel thankful that Mr. Cole is on my side.

"Thank you," I say in my *haha* voice.

Mr. Cole nods and continues, "So you haven't seen or heard from him since the accident, Sera?"

"No, sir. I don't know how to get ahold of him, and Dad brought me *here* for all of my medical treatment."

Dad says under his breath, "They have better care here. I've already told you that."

"Anyway," I continue, "I don't know if he was hurt. I hate not knowing. He probably thinks I just left him. It's awful really."

"And how old is Cal?"

"He's my age. We were both going to graduate in May," I say, tearing up. The wreck destroyed my plans, our plans. Not just getting through school but to be together. To see the world.

"I miss him so much," I say, wiping the tears that inevitably fall despite my attempt to stay strong.

"It's ok to cry, Sera. It sounds like you've been through a very rough time," Mr. Cole explains. "What injuries did you sustain?"

"I had to have my spleen removed. My legs were broken and my knee was torn up. I've been through multiple surgeries and a ton of rehab. Too much. But I want to get better even though I hate it. I still have to use this stupid cane to walk, but I was scared I wouldn't be able to walk at all for a while. It was horrible. I had to depend on everyone else to do things for me. I was stuck in a horrible hospital room and then an equally ugly and stifling rehab room."

"So are there things you were able to do before the accident that you can't do now? Obviously walking has been a struggle."

"Yeah. I don't think I will be able to walk without a limp, which is embarrassing, not to mention uncomfortable. My legs hurt sometimes, and my knee hurts most of the time, especially in the mornings when I get up and at night when I've been on it all day. I didn't get to graduate with my class. The school sent me a diploma in the mail. I haven't seen my friends in forever. I haven't done anything since the accident except stupid rehab and basic recovery. It has sucked so badly."

"Do you know if Cal had insurance, Sera? Or if he has had any other accidents in the past?"

"I'm not sure if he had insurance, but I assume he did. And I don't know for sure about any other wrecks, but he never mentioned any and his motorcycle seemed in good condition," I answer him. "I feel like I'm not much help. I just don't remember that much about that day. All I can say is that Cal is a good person, and he would have never done anything to put me in danger. Besides, Dad told me that the police report showed it to be the other man's fault."

"We will get copies of the police report and anything else we need for the case, but, if this goes to trial, we will need to know everything we can about both you and Cal. We want to be prepared for anything."

"Yes, Sir. Thank you."

After making a few more notes, Mr. Cole removes his glasses and looks up at my dad and me.

"Well, I think this is a good start. Is there anything else you can think of that I need to know?"

Shaking my head, I answer. "No."

Dad stands to his feet, seemingly unsatisfied with Mr. Cole's reaction to Cal and his involvement. Ready to leave, he says, "I think that covers it for now. I will meet with you again soon, Davis," shaking Mr. Cole's hand.

NOW

True to his word, Dad arrives to pick me up having so generously given me a whole night to wrap my life up here.

I answer the door at five minutes after noon, ready to stand my ground, but still feeling nervous because I hate any type of confrontation.

Last night, Mandy and I talked after Cal went home. She told me to *fake it until I make it* when I told her how scared I was. "You are old enough to be on your own, Sera. It's not like you are a 16-year-old runaway. Don't let him control you anymore. It sounds like he needs to get his priorities straight and go be with his wife. Either way, don't stress. I can be here if you want me to. I've never called in sick so I'm sure it won't be a problem," she told me.

"It's ok. I can handle it. I think it will be best for me to be alone. I even told Cal that. As much as I wish he could be here, I know it will be better for him to wait until Dad is gone. I just hope he will leave and not freak out on me too much," I answered her.

Dad stands at the doorway looking like he's ready for a fight if necessary, his lips thin with an agitated expression.

"Come in," I say, gesturing for him to enter with my hand. "Have a seat. Want anything to drink?" I ask, stalling.

"I'm fine, thank you. Are you all packed up?" He asks, looking around the room for the suitcases he expects to see.

"No," I say kind of quietly while sitting opposite him on the couch, my foot tucked under me. My t-shirt, shorts, and bare feet don't exactly speak travel apparel, at least in my father's upscale world, so I would assume he should be connecting the dots fairly quickly.

"What do you mean, 'no,' Sera?" he asks, sighing.

"I mean, I'm not going with you, Dad. I told you that I've built my life here. Things are good for me here, Dad. And Cal is here. We are together. I'm sorry if you don't like that, but it's the way it is. I'm 19, Dad, old enough to be on my own, and I promise I'm doing a good job."

"Sera, it's not about you doing a good job. There's no reason for you to be on your own. You need to live at home a little longer, go to college. Then, maybe, you will be ready to live on your own. You will have more time to heal and also more time to mature."

"I am mature, Dad," I say, feeling irritated.

"You're 19, Sera. You have no idea what this world is like. No idea. The fact that you are arguing with me about your maturity proves that. It's not easy to be a grown up; you really don't need to rush it."

"Ok. Well, I guess I'll learn as I go then. Plus, I have Cal to help me." I try to reason with him.

Dad grunts at the mention of Cal again. "Cal will hardly be of help to you, Sera. For one, he's not mature either. Two, it was his fault that you were hurt. I don't care whose fault the accident was. You should have never been on that bike with him. Hell, Sera, you shouldn't have been with him anyway. We talked about that. You knew how I felt about him," Dad says.

And it's my turn to grunt in frustration. "Dad," I say, raising my voice, "I'm sorry, ok? I'm freaking sorry I was with him without your blessing," I say, not even sure I really mean it. "But I couldn't let you dictate my life, Dad. I *love* him. I really, really, *really love him*. And I'm not leaving." I say, ending my rant.

A long pause creates the loudest silence ever, extending past this room, past this day, and into my future.

It's a little unnerving, so I can't help but speak, the need to fill in the gaps pressing.

"Dad, I spoke with Mr. Cole a couple of weeks ago."

"You spoke with Davis without me? Why, Sera? I thought you wanted my help in handling the case," he says, surprised.

"Because, when I got in touch with Cal, I told him about Mr. Cole. I asked him if he has a case, too, and he said that his mom had been trying to get him to talk to a lawyer but that he wasn't sure it was worth it. I told him that Mr. Cole is nice and helpful, and that I would be happy to go with him if he wanted to speak with him."

"So Cal went with you?"

"Yes. Actually, Mr. Cole met us here at a law office downtown. Cal's mom was there, too."

The expression on my father's face falls. I have to fight my natural reaction to comfort him so that I can maintain my strength. I will not go with him no matter what.

I continue, "Dad, it's ok. It was a good meeting. Cal is going to join our case, and Mr. Cole thinks that will actually make it stronger. He's even doing it on contingency for Cal since he believes this is a good case and a definite win. He set up a deposition for next week, here at that same office. You are welcome to come if you want to. Ok?"

Shrugging in defeat, Dad is noncommittal. "We'll see. I'm not happy about this, Sera. I don't want you making any decisions without me. Do you understand me? I'm leaving, but I'm not giving up. I still expect you to do what's right. I just hope you are *mature* enough to recognize it." He stands to leave. "I'll let myself out."

I don't even say goodbye. As soon as the door closes, I say out loud, "Whatever, Dad. I'll freaking show you *mature*." I yell and hit the couch cushion beside me, anger winding through me like wildfire.

"It's ok, Cal. We'll do this together. I'm nervous, too, but the accident wasn't our fault, so I'm sure there is nothing they can say that will hurt us. Ok?"

Nodding back to me, Cal and I walk arm in arm into the law office where the deposition is to be held. I walk on Cal's right side, Luke on his left. He's had Luke with him more often recently. He said he didn't want to rely on anyone, even me, to help him, and that he still needs to get used to walking with Luke in unfamiliar places.

I had only met Cal's mom once before when we met with Mr. Cole, so it's nice to see her again. Her brown wavy hair hangs a little too long over her eyes, but she pushes it back causing a curtain-look down the middle as each side drapes carefully across her forehead before falling down around her ears. Her thin frame and worn face reveal a hard life, but the laugh lines around her eyes also reflect contentment and happiness, especially when she is next to Cal. She seems extremely nice, having encouraged both of us before sitting in a chair pulled back from the table a little, as if to give us space.

Mr. Cole is already in the room, as is another attorney, presumably representing the defendant, who is not present.

A court reporter sits at the end of the table with a recording device and some sort of machine on which she can quickly type everything that is said, and a videographer stands in one corner setting up equipment.

After making acquaintances, Cal and I sit quietly in the chairs opposite the attorneys and wait quietly for the deposition to begin.

The defense attorney, Jim Witt, asks, "We're starting with Cal, right?" looking between Mr. Cole and Cal and me. Nodding our heads, Mr. Cole confirms. "Ok, let's get started," motioning to the videographer and the court reporter.

The court reporter is first to speak. "Mr. Stevens, raise your right hand," she says to Cal. "Do you swear to tell the truth, the whole truth, and nothing but the truth, so help you God?"

"I do," Cal states.

Mr. Witt asks, "Will you please state your name for the record?"

"Cal Stevens."

"May I call you Cal?"

"Yes, sir."

"My name is Jim Witt, and I represent Lancaster Plumbing and their employee who was driving the truck that was involved in this accident. Do you understand who I am and what my role is here?"

"Yes, sir," Cal answers again.

"Have you ever given a deposition before?"

"No, sir."

"Well, I'd like to go over just a few ground rules. Are you aware that your testimony here is given under oath and it's subject to perjury just the same as if you were testifying in court before a judge and a jury?"

"Ok."

"Be sure to answer audibly so the court reporter can take it down. Try to wait until I finish asking my question before you answer so that we aren't talking over each other. If I ask any question that you don't understand, please ask me to rephrase it. If you need a break at any time, just let me know."

Finished with the rules, he places his hands together on top of his notepad, prepared. "Alright, let's go ahead and get started. Tell me about where you were born and raised as well as your educational background," Mr. Witt says.

Before Cal can answer, my dad steps into the room and takes a seat near Cal's mom. Mr. Cole speaks to my father, "Come on in, Henry. Have a seat. We're just getting started."

Cal takes a deep breath and begins. "I was born in Santa Fe, New Mexico, but my Mother moved us here shortly after that when I was one year old to be near my grandfather who ended up passing away with cancer a year later. We've been here ever since, living in various duplexes and apartments. I attended Cresthaven Elementary, Wilkerson Middle School, and Lincoln High. I graduated last May, at least on paper, since the wreck happened a couple of weeks before."

"I understand that was your motorcycle. How long had you had it?"

"Well, I was able to get a job at Frank's automotive when I was only 14, just doing odd jobs, so I saved money. When I turned 16, after I got my driver's license, I bought a cheap junker car from my boss. I saved up for a couple more years; so, when I was 18, I traded in my car and paid cash to buy the bike. I took a motorcycle class and got my motorcycle license right before buying it."

"How long did you have your motorcycle license before you had the accident?"

"Almost eight months, sir."

"Had you ever had any other motorcycle accidents?" Mr. Witt asks.

"No, sir."

"Did you ever have any car accidents?"

"No, sir."

"Let's talk about the day of the accident. Where were you going when the accident occurred?"

Grimacing, I feel myself tense just thinking about that day.

"We were going to my apartment to study," Cal answers.

"And where were you coming from?"

"We were coming from Sera's house."

"Did you see the truck before it hit you?" Mr. Witt asks.

"I can't remember. I don't think so."

"What *do* you remember about the accident?"

"Not a lot. We were driving down Main. It was only about 5 miles to my house from hers."

I notice Cal push his sunglasses up on his nose as if to hide his tears.

"Sera was on the back, and I remember her laughing. She loved to ride with me." He pauses before adding, "Then the next thing I remember was being on the ground. I just remember thinking about Sera. I wasn't sure exactly what was happening, but she wasn't with me anymore."

Cal visibly flinches when he hears me sniffle beside him. I can't help the tears that fall as I hear about his grief, and especially about his memories of that day.

"Do you need a break?" Mr. Witt asks, noticing Cal is upset.

"No, sir. I want to get this over with," Cal says.

"Now I'm not trying to be offensive, but I need to know whether or not you had any alcohol to drink within 24 hours before that, or if you took prescription drugs or illegal drugs?"

"I didn't do drugs and I didn't drink anything for more than 24 hours before the accident."

"I understand that you lost your sight. Can you tell me about your injuries?" Mr. Witt asks Cal.

I cringe just thinking about how horrifying this has all been. What we both lost has devastated us. Grabbing Cal's hand, I hope to reassure him that we are in this together. I want him to feel my love for him and know that I'm here for him. He squeezes it and seems to relax before answering.

"I stayed in the hospital with a traumatic brain injury and a few broken bones for three long months. Was in a coma for over a week I think. I basically had to learn how to do everything all over again, just without being able to see. You would be surprised at how many things we don't realize are much easier with sight. Just walking down a hall, I had to have help. Picking out clothes, taking a shower, getting around, all of it is different now."

"What are your plans now?"

All of a sudden, Cal becomes upset, abruptly saying, "I'll take that break now." After being dismissed, he stands up so that we can walk into the hall, our lawyer following.

Mr. Cole says, "You're doing great, Cal. Just relax. It's almost over, and then it will be Sera's turn. Sera, you remember when I asked you questions? It will be just like that. You will both be fine."

I hug Cal's side, his arm around me. "I love you," I whisper to him. He answers with a kiss on the top of my head.

His mom hands us each a bottle of water. "Got these in the room. I think they're free," she says.

I don't see my father; I guess he stayed behind in the deposition room.

After about fifteen minutes, Mr. Cole escorts us back into the room.

Mr. Witt says, "Ok. Do you feel alright, Cal? Are you ready to continue?"

"Yes, sir," Cal answers.

"Ok, so let's get back to it. What are your plans now, Cal?"

"Well, my plans are pretty much shot to hell now, aren't they? Sera and I were going to travel around the US on my bike. Not only can I not ride my motorcycle anymore, but I thought Sera was dead. I had no idea that she had gone to Dallas until she came back recently. I'm going to school and working on an art degree, but it isn't what I had planned. And the worst part...I can't ever see Sera again. I mean, sure, I can be around her, with her, but I can't see her. I can't see anything. Colors, trees, clouds. I miss it. I miss seeing her."

I never told my father about my plans with Cal. His reaction makes me flinch, his clinched teeth and cold stare at Cal and then at me.

Mr. Witt says, "On that note, why don't we move on to taking Sera's deposition?"

After swearing in, Mr. Witt went through many of the same questions with me. I tried not to look at my father. I could feel his anger with me anyway, though, unfortunately.

It's when Mr. Witt asks me about my plans that Dad audibly sighs.

"As Cal said, we were going to leave after graduation to travel and explore the United States." I look at my father while answering. "Cal and I love each other. We were excited to be together. To spend time together. To grow up together. But the accident took that from us. We will never be able to see the world. When I was behind Cal on his bike, it was the most free I've ever felt in my life, and now I feel like we've been imprisoned by our injuries. By our circumstances. We still plan to be together. We are both going to college, and I hope to use what happened to help others. But it's still not the same. I can forgive, but I can't forget. I just want to start fresh, *without* interference of any kind," I say, hoping Dad understands.

My father looks down at his hands in his lap.

Mr. Witt thanks us and gets up to leave, explaining he has to hurry to make his flight home. Cal and I speak with his mom while preparing to exit the room, and my father is talking to Mr. Cole.

Once outside, we stand by the car waiting for everyone to come out. I want to talk to Mr. Cole before he leaves to find out what's next.

"That went well. We'll be looking at mediation unless they make an offer first. I'll be in touch with you soon," Mr. Cole says.

"Sounds good. Thank you for your help," I tell him.

Cal follows, "Yes, thank you, sir. I appreciate everything you've done not only for me but for Sera." Shaking his hand, Mr. Cole turns to leave, waving at my father on his way to his car.

My father approaches us. "Can I speak with you privately for a moment, Sera?" I agree, walking towards my father's car, leaving Cal with his Mom.

"Dad..."

Before I can continue, my father embraces me. I'm surprised, and maybe a little wary, but I'm thankful. I haven't hugged my father in a very long time. It feels good.

"Sera, I can't say that I'm not extremely disappointed that you lied to me about your plans, and quite frankly, even though I hate how it happened, I'm thankful your plans were thwarted. You need to go to college. Travelling is something you can do later, when you have your education behind you. And while I'm still not happy about your relationship with Cal, I'm going to try to accept that you are living on your own and staying here. I can see that you won't be convinced to leave with me, especially after watching the two of you in there today. I'm sorry I've implied you were immature. I just love you too much to let you go," he says, breaking up. The tears in my eyes threaten to spill as he talks more openly with me than he has in a long time.

"I'm your Dad, Sera. I care about you. I know this has been hard for you, and I've been critical, but you took it into your own hands. You handled talking to the lawyer, and you were very good in there, Sera. Your mother would be so proud of you. If she were here, she probably would have kicked me by now," he says, chuckling through his own tears.

"I love you, Dad. Thank you for loving me. And thank you for trusting me. Finally!" I say, teasing. "How about Megan? Have you seen her or heard from her lately?" I ask, worried about him.

"No. Not really."

"You should talk to her, Dad. I know she loves you. She told me before I left, and I *might* have been texting her lately," I say, smiling.

"You have, huh? Well, that surprises me and also gives me hope. You know, I always wanted you two to have a closer relationship, but I understood she couldn't replace your mother."

"She's actually pretty great. It took me a long time to allow myself to see it, and I feel badly about that, but at least I see it now. Go, Dad.

225

I've got things under control here. You go take care of you. And Megan."

"Isn't it backwards for the daughter to give the father relationship advice?" he asks, smiling.

"Maybe, but it's happening, so get moving," I urge him in a silly voice. Giving him one last hug, I make my way back to Cal.

My love. My hope. My future.

CHAPTER 31

Beautifully wrapped gifts wait below the 9 foot Christmas tree decorated in gold and red. Though I've never wanted for anything physical, my mother's absence is always more prevalent during the holidays. It makes me sad for Megan this year. I've never tried to look at it from her perspective, and she obviously tries too hard to make the day special.

This year, as we have every year, we eat a full breakfast using our fine china before joining together in the living room to exchange gifts. Among other clothes, Megan got me a gorgeous cashmere sweater. My father bought me a beautiful necklace and earring set from James Avery. He also gave Megan jewelry, which I think she likes.

Since I haven't wanted to venture out to shop, I bought my gifts online. It's hard to choose a gift for someone who can afford everything, so when I found some personalized and unique things on Etsy, I was thrilled. Megan's expression when she opens my gift to her is priceless. It is a silver necklace, on it a round charm with a glass globe cover that says, "Thank you for raising me as your own, Love, Sera."

With tears in her eyes, she hugs me for over a minute, thanking me and telling me how much she loves it.

"I'm glad you like it, Megan. Now it's your turn, Dad," I say, smiling.

Upon unwrapping his gift, my Dad quietly looked through the pages of the photo album full of all my favorite photos spanning my entire life.

"How did you do this?" He asks, tearing up.

"I've been working on it since I've been home. I was able to scan the pictures in and create the book online. Do you like it?"

"I love it, honey. I can't believe you found all of these pictures. It's great," he says, grinning at certain pictures. The one of me in a bathtub with overflowing bubbles makes him laugh.

Moments like these bring tears to my eyes. I will miss my father and Megan. Trying to take control of the anxiety that sneaks its way into my heart, I take a couple of deep breaths and attempt to still my wringing hands.

Megan smiles a sad smile at me, understanding my apprehension, but before my Dad has a chance to notice, I quickly rally my feelings with an internal pep talk.

It's going to be ok. I want this. I need this. I'm just going home.

NOW

"You didn't tell me you actually applied for school," Cal says from the passenger seat of my Bronco. "I thought you were still just thinking about it."

"I was going to surprise you."

"Do you know what you want to major in yet?" he asks me.

"I'm not sure, but I was kind of thinking about studying to be a therapist of some sort. I spent so much time in rehab, I feel like I kind of have a good start. Plus, I really loved all of the patients who were there with me. People need someone who not only knows how to work with them physically, but someone who cares.

Someone who is encouraging and loving. I feel like I could be that person."

"I don't know if I ever told you, but one of the main things that attracted me to you is your light. You glow, Sera. And I realize that sounds kind of weird, but you are bright. People are drawn to you. It's something I missed so deeply, and even when you came back, I mourned my loss of sight all over again. But then I realized, like a light bulb came on in my head, that your light is not something I see with my eyes, but rather through your heart and soul. You are truly beautiful, Sera, and I believe that whatever you decide to pursue will be good."

"Cal..." I can't even respond. Wiping my tears, I reach over to take his hand. "I love you so much."

"I love you, too, babe, but what the hell is wet on your hand?" he says, chuckling.

"Oh my gosh." Taking my hand away to wipe it on my jeans, I laugh. "My happy tears; that's all."

"I'm just teasing you," he says, continuing to laugh.

After the deposition, we decided to go back to where everything started. Parking in the gravelly lot, Cal says, "You know, I came here once after the accident. I was alone and it was heartbreaking, yet peaceful."

"Was it hard to find your way?" I ask him. We haven't talked much about our injuries, perhaps a means to forget our struggles and embrace our future. I have to admit, I have a lot of questions I want to ask Cal. Losing sight must be challenging and dispiriting.

"That's a hard question. I've had to learn so many new ways to do things, to manage my new life. Coming here was my first time out alone. I took a bus for the first time with a nice, but very talkative, bus driver," he says, remembering with a chuckle. "She directed me towards the water, and I just listened for the waves before turning right since I remembered where our tree was. It was different. Weird and uncomfortable, but it also made me feel empowered, and closer to you."

"Gosh, I can't imagine. It's weird how we can take things for granted. I mean, I couldn't walk for over a month, and even when I started again, it was almost like I was a baby relearning each step. Then I couldn't drive or do anything independently. It totally sucked."

"That's exactly what bothered me the most, too, other than losing you, of course. The loss of independence. Depending on my mother to pick my clothes is true blind faith."

Giggling at his pun and at the idea of his having to rely on his mom for deciding his wardrobe, I concur. "So, what is it like? Can you see anything at all?"

"Nope. Pitch black. Sucks ass, but I *can* appreciate my new Spidey senses," he jokes, laughing.

"Seriously? Are your other senses more noticeable now?"

"They are."

Stopping at our tree, we sit on the blanket I brought from home.

Cal says, "Lie down next to me."

"Ok," I answer.

"Now close your eyes. What do you hear?" He asks.

Smiling, I listen for a minute. "I hear the water. Birds. A bug. Ooooh, a duck quacking," I add excitedly.

"Now, what do you smell?"

"Ummm, grass, the pond, you." I turn to face him, opening my eyes.

"Close your eyes, Sera."

"Dang it. How did you know I opened them? It's not like you could hear or smell that," I say, laughing.

"I just know you, and you are impatient," he tells me. Closing my eyes again, I lie on the blanket, waiting for his next direction.

"What do you feel, Sera?"

"The breeze?" I ask, unsure of where he's going with this. But as soon as I ask, he runs his fingers over my chest just below my neck.

"Oh God. I feel your touch."

"Where?"

"On my chest."

"Now where?" he asks.

"My hair...my tummy...my arms." I hear him shift but keep my eyes closed. It's erotic and interesting at the same time.

His lips touch mine softly. "How about now?" he whispers, his face just above my own.

"Mmmm." His chuckle gives me tingles.

"Now?" he asks, his lips moving to my stomach.

"Oh God."

Warmth fills me, his touch igniting my own senses.

"This," he says, "is what I feel." He continues to caress me. "I feel love. I smell love. I touch, and taste love when I'm with you, and that's all that fucking matters."

"Cal..."

My words are consumed. Our souls fused.

One.

Where light and dark collide, vibrant colors paint the world, creating a beauty that truly can't be explained. The perfection of a sunrise awakens a love so complete, that each night, the sunset reveals its glory.

And God seems more real than ever before.

EPILOGUE

The lake is calm today. Luke has learned the area and enjoys playing near the water. He's great at warning Cal of each fallen branch, tall brush, tree stump.

"It's finished. Will you come look?" he asks me.

"Yay. I'm so excited. I hate how you've kept me in the dark."

Taking his hand, we walk alongside Luke back into the house to Cal's art room. A three-foot clay sculpture poses on the work table, as if waiting for praise, approval.

"It's beautiful, Cal," I whisper, my hand covering my mouth as an expression of awe.

The collection of angels he made when he first started sculpting remain in the art building for all to see, cherished. I love them all.

But this.

This is spectacular, the huge wings in flight, gorgeous instruments of freedom, giving refuge to the seraph bearing them.

"It's you, baby. My Serafina."

"I love it. And I love you." Entwined, we embrace for several minutes, at peace.

The loud knock at the door of our lake house finally separates us.

With the extremely large settlement Cal and I each received, we purchased the place where we first united completely.

"I'll get it," I tell him.

Mandy and Ray are first to arrive, announcing proudly that they brought beer for the party.

"Dude, people don't drink beer at baby showers," I laugh, teasing Mandy.

"The guys do. They can hang out outside. This is a celebration for girls only."

"Oh, ok then," I respond, acknowledging her authority on the matter.

My dad and Megan show up shortly after, thankfully doing well. My father took Megan on a second honeymoon once Cal and I announced our engagement. He said he didn't want to wait any longer to express his love and admiration for Megan.

Wearing my mother's vintage wedding dress, Cal and I married in May on the second anniversary of our accident, revising that date forever in our minds to be a joyful one. It was the most beautiful spring day. Not quite summer yet, the warm weather wasn't too hot. Joined by our friends and family, we finally realized our dream of being together officially, without any barriers. The fragrant flowers alongside the chairs leading up to a white arch near the lake subtly and naturally brightened the atmosphere, creating the perfect place for unity.

Finally arriving for today's gathering, Cal's Mom and her date join the group, also including several other friends and family.

"So, how long has this been going on?" Cal asks his Mom after she announces her boyfriend and herself.

"Umm, maybe a year?" his mom answers, nervously.

"Wow, and you hid it from me? Why?"

"I wasn't sure if it might be conflict of interest. And you were doing so well with him. I guess I might as well tell you; we are engaged."

Before Cal can respond, his therapist, Dr. Roberts, takes Cal's hand to shake it. "I hope you understand, Cal. Your mother means so much to me."

"Sure, I understand. And quite frankly, I'm thankful. I think you will both be happy together," he says, pulling him in for a side hug. "Now I can get my therapy for free, right?" He asks, chuckling.

Dr. Roberts replies, "Sure, as long as you do what I say," also laughing.

Cal's Mom says, "I talked to Dr. Roberts during that time, too. He helped me a lot after everything happened. You know how hard it was for me to see you hurting, Cal. And Bill here," she says, grabbing his hand, "encouraged me to pray. You know, I think this all happened for a reason. Your artwork would have never happened if it weren't for this change in your life. And even though it took a while, you reunited with Sera. It's a beautiful life, Cal."

"Thanks, Mom. It's still hard sometimes, but you're probably right. I can't see how God would purposely take my sight, but I do think things are working for good now. Remember telling me about that, *Bill?*" Cal asks, laughing at using his first name, but also sounding appreciative of his help and encouragement during such a dark time.

"I sure do, Cal. Now, where's that pretty girl of yours? I still haven't met her you know."

After introducing Dr. Roberts to me, Cal and I take our spots together near the fireplace in the living room. We have done some decorating to the old place. The living room now boasts a more comfortable, leather couch and chair with a beautiful, fluffy beige rug adorning the hardwood floor. The lamps brighten the room, but I love to keep the curtains open during the day to allow the natural light inside. Cal has his own studio in one room of the house, and the third bedroom is newly painted with a gorgeous cherry wood crib waiting in the corner near a rocking chair. I can't wait to fill the room, and our home, with the wonderful miracle inside of me.

Addressing the group of loved ones, I say, "This is great. I'm so thankful you could all be here with us to celebrate. I know you have all been waiting for us to tell you the name and the sex of the baby, and I think we finally decided on the perfect one."

Looking at Cal, the smile on his lips reflects his pride, his hand cradling the growing bump on my belly.

"HER NAME... IS WILLOW ROSE."

ACKNOWLEDGMENTS

I would like to thank the following people: My husband, Jeremy, for working two jobs while going to school, being a great dad and husband, and for loving and supporting me throughout this process; my mom, Linda, for her encouragement, editing and help with formatting; my daughter-in-law, Leahnna, who read and gave me great feedback; my friend, Kim, for her detailed encouragement and feedback; my knowledgeable and sweet author friend, Amy Van Horn, for beta reading and giving me helpful advice and support; my son, Isaac, for drawing the awesome and cool picture used on the cover; my friend Beth for designing the first cover; Kat Mellon, for designing the awesome second cover; my cousin, Angie, for her mad editing skills; Kerby and Jordan, for their beautiful faces on the cover; and my 9 children, who are my inspiring wild bunch.

Thank You, God, for giving me the words to write this novel. I pray that You will bless it and that it will be used to reach many, many people.

ABOUT THE AUTHOR

Elisa Ellis was born and raised in a small West Texas town. She married her high school sweetheart, Jeremy, and together, they raise their nine children. She briefly taught high school English before deciding to stay home with her kiddos, and has enjoyed a passion for photography and for writing. She currently proofreads court transcripts while continuing to write.

Interact with Elisa on:
    Facebook
    Goodreads
    Key Proofreading

Purchase Elisa's first novel here:
    Linked, We Soar

www.ingramcontent.com/pod-product-compliance
Lightning Source LLC
Chambersburg PA
CBHW031317170626
46807CB00002B/450